He was hunter.

She was prey.

She caught a quick glimpse outlined in the bright moonlight of a big man, densely muscled. At least he was shaped like a man. But his eyes belonged to a hungry, hunting beast. Fire burned in those eyes, the deep red of glowing coals. The anguish in them was terrifying. His gaze caught and held her even as he bore down on her too swiftly for her to escape. . . .

"Susan Sizemore enraptures readers, securing her rightful place among the writers who will soon rise to the top. . . ."

—*Romantic Times*

Praise for
I Burn for You

"With her new twist on ancient vampire lore, Sizemore creates an excellent and utterly engaging new world. *I Burn for You* is sexy, exciting, and just plain thrilling. It's the perfect start for a hot, new series."

—*Romantic Times*

"I adored *I Burn for You* and really hope it's the beginning of another wonderful vampire series from Ms. Sizemore."

—*Old Book Barn Gazette*

"Sizemore has long worn two writing hats, that of romance author and sf-fantasy scribe, and . . . the bonding of [her] two literary worlds is as powerful as what Alex and Domini feel for each other in this sexy read laced with laughter, the first in a burning new series."

—*Booklist*

"Sizemore's hunky vamps can visit me anytime! I was so sorry to see this book end. This one is a must buy."

—*All About Romance*

More raves for the work of Susan Sizemore

"Wicked sensuality."

—Christina Dodd

"Ms. Sizemore's breed of vampire is intriguing and her delivery compelling."

—*Romantic Times*

"Thrilling, sexually charged."

—*Booklist*

"Sizemore knows how to write realistic vampires."

—*All about Romance Review*

Also by Susan Sizemore

I Thirst for You

SUSAN SIZEMORE

POCKET STAR BOOKS

NEW YORK LONDON TORONTO SYDNEY

A Pocket Star Book published by
POCKET BOOKS, a division of Simon & Schuster, Inc.
1230 Avenue of the Americas, New York, NY 10020

This book is a work of fiction. Names, characters, places and incidents are products of the author's imagination or are used fictitiously. Any resemblance to actual events or locales or persons, living or dead, is entirely coincidental.

Copyright © 2004 by Susan Sizemore

ISBN-13: 978-1-4165-2354-3
ISBN-10:   1-4165-2354-5

This Pocket Star Books paperback edition April 2006

10   9   8   7   6   5   4   3   2   1

POCKET STAR BOOKS and colophon are registered trademarks of Simon & Schuster, Inc.

Cover illustration by Tom Hallman

Manufactured in the United States of America

For information regarding special discounts for bulk purchases, please contact Simon & Schuster Special Sales at 1-800-456-6798 or business@simonandschuster.com.

For Micki Nuding. Great editors inspire,
and Micki, that book you sent me
was truly inspirational!

I Thirst
for You

Chapter One

Two things pain can do for you: sharpen you up or dull you down. It never does anything for your mood. He'd been in pain for over a week, and the crystal clarity he'd run on was dulling down to shards of scoured glass. He'd been running on adrenaline, when he needed blood. That had to change—soon—if he was going to survive. Blood was survival.

If he survived long enough out here, once he was free he could start thinking about revenge. He *yearned* to think about what he'd do to those who'd imprisoned him—but letting those thoughts surface could easily lead to hallucinations, a sure way to get himself caught again.

"Not going to happen," he growled, the sound a rumble of thunder in the desert night. The name of the game was survival, and survival meant paring himself down to pure animal instinct.

Blood.

That was the only order of business.

He crouched on the ground, where scorpions scurried to get out of his way, rested his hands on the thick base of a saguaro cactus, and concentrated on finding blood. Animal blood wouldn't do; it had to be human. Preferably female.

He could hear the soft breathing of doves nesting in the cactus. Bats fluttered and flitted overhead, and he could hear their sonar squeaks piercing the air. Hearts beat all around him, so many small living things going about their nocturnal business. He was surrounded by life, but had never been so alone.

He blocked out everything else and searched for the one heartbeat that had to be out there. *Had* to be waiting for him. When the need was the greatest, that was when you found The One. Wasn't that how the old myth went?

Eventually his head came up, then turned, nostrils flaring.

"Son of a bitch," he muttered.

A slow smile creased his pain-ravaged features. He rose, gave a quick look up at the full moon, and whispered an ancient word of thanks.

Then he turned south and ran, spending all his remaining energy in a burst of desperate speed.

The stars were huge overhead, and the moon rode high in the sky. Stevie Nicks's voice was in her ears, singing about sorcerers and sapphires. Maybe she should have been enjoying the deep silence of the desert night, but she preferred the music coming through the headphones of her Discman as she lay on a sleeping bag outside her tent and drank in the vast emptiness.

She'd always liked being alone, but since the plane crash she craved privacy more than ever. She'd been called brave and heroic, and she hated that. She'd been the pilot, and she survived—which seemed so *wrong* to her. The admiration made her cringe; so did the sympathy. She hoped the solitude would be healing.

She'd always absorbed other people's emotions too easily, and it was worse now, since her head injury when the plane hit the ground. The physical wound had closed, but her mind was still open. Things poured into it, thoughts and emotions, things that had nothing to do with her. She used to be able to control it most of the time. "Empath," a witchy friend had called her once, a Sensitive.

Once it had been kind of fun to have this psychic ability; now it made her a fugitive. Now the need to be alone was the reason she'd camped out in the national forest south of Tucson. Here, she had some peace from the joys and pains and hungers that didn't belong to her.

Right now she concentrated on the music to get away from the pain that *did* belong to her. Four people had died in the plane crash. Four others had lived besides her, but lives saved didn't make up for the guilt of lives lost. No one called it pilot error; it had been a freak storm. Wind shear. Lightning. An act of God. But she should have . . .

Something. There must have been something she could have done.

Try not to think about it. Try to move on. She'd heard those words so many times. But where did you move on to when by all rights you should be dead?

Maybe she *was* dead, and hell was having to hide away from the rest of the human race to keep from—

Hell? You don't know anything about hell.

The thought raced out of the night, straight into her heart, like an avalanche with a New York accent.

Then hunger shot through her, hunger that was a burning pain that set her writhing on the ground and clawing feverishly at the earth. It absorbed her, nauseated her, leaving her twisted up in a sweating, cringing ball when the pain withdrew. Gradually she realized that the pain was not hers . . . but that it was coming for her.

And she realized she did *not* want to die. In that way, the rising fear was a gift.

Terror pumped adrenaline through her, bringing her to her feet, and she turned to run from the unknown danger.

And found that she had turned toward the very thing she feared, as he came rushing at her like a runaway freight train out of the night.

She caught a quick glimpse in the bright moonlight of a big man, densely muscled. At least, he was shaped like a man. But his eyes belonged to a hungry, hunting beast. Fire burned in those eyes, the deep red of glowing coals, and the anguish in them was terrifying.

The woman's fear speared him, but he kept on coming. He had no choice: he was hunter, she was prey. He felt her pain when she pivoted and twisted her ankle trying to escape him. She ran despite the sprain; instinct made him follow.

After being pursued so long, being the pursuer brought him pinpricks of pride, and pleasure. He almost remembered what it felt like to be Prime.

It was a short chase. He followed the pounding of her heart and quick, sobbing breaths a few yards, then grasped her around the waist and brought her to the ground. They landed in the spiky shoots of a yucca, but he pulled her out before any cactus spines penetrated her skin. Her blood belonged to him—every drop—and how he took it was under *his* control.

Another time he might enjoy subduing her struggles, but he didn't have time to waste with love play. He was growing weaker.

He carried her back and sank to his knees onto a sleeping bag in front of her tent.

He ripped off her loose-fitting shirt while she fought and scratched at him. He was aware of her surprise when he didn't go for her bra or try to rip off her pants. He stroked a thumb down her long, lean throat, feeling her blood like blue heat beneath the satin skin, loving the strong, fast pulse. His fangs were already out, had been hard in his mouth for days.

He pushed her down and fell on top of her. Her scream punctured what remained of the shielding that protected his mind, and her fear drove through him like a stake. Shock sent him into her mind. He found psychic injury, a torn-open place that left her nearly helpless all the time.

He pulled out quickly, unwilling to take more from her mind than he must. And at least he could ease this for her—so there would be a give as well as take.

He drilled a thought into her head and made sure she understood.

Then he forgot about everything but need. He kissed the side of her throat once, because he could not bear to make this intimate act completely impersonal. Then he sank his fangs into her. His need was so desperate, he couldn't make the bleeding a slow, sensual sipping. What he did brought her to powerful orgasm within a moment.

It brought him life, and he drank and drank and drank.

Chapter Two

Jo Elliot woke up not sure what had happened but, even semiconscious, knowing it was *not* a bad dream. It was real, as real as the crash, and just as life-changing. Though her hazy mind couldn't focus, but her body was deeply aware of that.

She gradually recognized the cooing of doves, a sound she'd always loved. Then the buzz of an airplane engine in the distance. She recognized the make of the motor.

Very nearby she heard the sound of breathing—not just her own, but someone else's, whose breaths were unnaturally slow and deep.

And there was weight on her, hot and heavy against her thighs and hips and across her chest. She didn't want to open her eyes; she didn't really want to see what held her down. Skin pressed to hers, sweat to sweat. His face was next to hers, it was his breath that sounded in her ear.

He had come out of the night, and he had . . .

She didn't know what he had done. Whatever it was, she felt weak. Used. Her bones were melted, and her brain was fried. She felt hungover and hard-ridden, but—

She had no memory of rape; no memory of pain. Yet *something* had happened. And she knew he wanted more.

She didn't want the new day to begin, because a totally new reality waited for her. Because he wasn't going to let her go.

"That's right," Marcus Cage said. He lifted his mind from her surface thoughts and his head from her shoulder. He looked at her, knowing she deliberately kept her eyes closed, not wanting to see what the monster looked like. Thanks to last night's feasting, his fangs were under control and safely sheathed once more. He looked like a man, but he felt like hell.

It was a few minutes after dawn. He wanted to get out of the growing light, but he took a few moments to study his captive. She had short blond hair and fine-boned features, with a short, sharp nose, high cheekbones, and a stubborn, square chin. She was on the skinny side, with breasts smaller than he liked, but he admired her long, slender neck. Marc was definitely a neck man.

But he didn't need sentimentality to memorize his beloved's features. Now that he had her blood in him, he could find her at the bottom of a pitch-black mine shaft during a total eclipse. And he didn't have time to waste on anything, not even on letting her get used to the idea of his being there.

He took her by the shoulders and gently shook her. "Look at me," he ordered. "Get used to me. I'm not going away."

Her captor's deep, rumbling voice penetrated Jo's mind, and his touch sent a bolt of electricity through her. Suddenly she was almost as angry as she was afraid, and her eyes flew open.

"Get off me!"

"Fine."

He got up and pulled her to her feet after him. Standing, Jo had to keep looking up to look him in the eyes. He was very big, with a hard-muscled body. He'd obviously spent a lot of time pumping iron. In a prison exercise yard, was her guess. His body was magnificent, but a heavy jaw and large nose spoiled any chance of his ever being called handsome. He looked like a thug, but there was something about his full-lipped, sensual mouth and the expression in his dark brown eyes that belied the initial impression of his being a monster.

A beast that thinks, she thought; a beast that feels.

"That still makes me a beast," he said.

A beast that reads minds?

His huge hand was across her mouth before he involuntary scream came out. His other arm was around her, holding her to his chest. She was aware of the sharp male tang of his sweat and the heat coming off of him in almost visible waves. It was barely past dawn, yet his slightly olive skin was already starting to burn.

She could almost, not quite, feel his pain. It wasn't anything like last night. He had himself under control now, but it was like a wild animal straining on a leash. It could get loose again. She became very still, afraid of provoking that animal.

"I'm going to let you go," he said. "And you're not going to run."

He wasn't asking, he wasn't threatening, it was a statement of fact. Jo didn't even bother with nodding agreement. When he stepped back she stayed put, oddly aware of his absence.

She was trying not to think about his reading her mind. Marc almost chuckled, but knew that a normal person running into the paranormal coped with the weirdness any way they could. He'd be sympathetic if he had the time, and if this woman was a normal mortal. She was probably one of those psychics who pretended they weren't different. That kind of virgin was fun to court under normal circumstances, but right now there was no time for anything cute or coy.

"You belong to me," he gave her the flat-out truth. "What's your name?"

He looked around to see if anything among her camping gear would be useful. The light hurt him—and he needed to feed again as soon as she could tolerate it, so they had to get to somewhere sheltered quickly.

"Do you have a gun?" he asked. "A knife? Do you know what could happen to a woman alone out here?"

"Jo. Yes. No. You," she answered his questions in the order he'd asked.

"Where's the gun?"

She pointed toward the bright blue Jeep Cherokee Sport parked beyond the small tent.

"Pack up," he said as he headed toward the Jeep.

"What do you mean, 'pack up'?" she called after him.

He turned to face her outrage. "It's your stuff," he told her. "I don't know what to do with it." He couldn't help but smile at her. "Or do you expect me to be a gentleman and do all the heavy lifting?"

"I expect you to steal my car and go," she said. "Just—leave. Okay?"

She looked really pretty when she was angry as hell, with the sun shining in her golden hair. He also liked that she was standing up to him. It was too bad he couldn't do what she wanted.

He came back to her and held out his hand. "Forgot the keys."

She fished them out of her pants pocket and slapped them in his palm. "Go."

"Pack up," he repeated.

He found a 9mm Beretta in the storage compartment between the front seats. He came back to where she was folding up the tent, the weapon in his belt. "You probably think that if you'd had this with you last night, it would have done you some good," he told her. "It wouldn't have."

Jo pretended to ignore him as she finished with her gear, but she was all too aware of him. She could feel the intensity of his dark eyes on her as she moved and knew she wasn't imagining it.

When she bent to roll up the sleeping bag, she saw a couple of white buttons lying on it, and she realized that her shirt was hanging open. A vague memory stirred. There were a few brownish specks on the bag as well, where her head had been not so long ago. Drops of dried blood? Jo put a hand to her throat. Her neck was aching—because she'd slept on it funny, right?

Even as she made this logical excuse, she turned on her captor. "You bit me!"

He answered with the faintest of gestures with a hand that moved far too gracefully for someone of his size. "Hurry up," was all he said. "Forget the tent."

"What?"

"Do it."

Jo knelt beside her clothing duffel and quickly shrugged off the ruined shirt, then pulled a Hysteria tour T-shirt over her head. The screaming face on the black background certainly suited the situation. There was no way she was going to change anything more than her shirt in front of this man, even though she was grungy and sweaty and—

"You're not the only one who needs a shower. Come on."

"Stop that!" she snapped. *He's not really reading my mind. He's just reading body language, making obvious guesses.* "And give me a hand if you're in such a hurry," she added.

He sauntered away from the Jeep and took the sleeping bag in one hand.

Jo kept the duffel. When he moved to the back of the Jeep, she fished the spare keys out of the duffel's side pocket and sprinted for the driver's-side door.

"Cute," was his comment when he appeared in front of her and snatched the keys from her hand.

Her momentum caused her to run hard into his big, broad body. It was like hitting a wall. She bounced back and landed flat on her butt on the rocky ground. She could read no expression on his face as he loomed above her for long, menacing seconds; but her own terror brought up images of his brutalizing her for daring to attempt escape. The unnatural speed with which he'd intercepted her added to her fear.

When he reached down, she flinched and tried to scramble away. He picked her up and hauled her over his shoulder as if she were light as meringue. The ease with which he handled her was as shocking as his speed. Okay, he was a big guy and she'd lost weight after the crash, but she wasn't a feather.

He carried her to the Jeep and put her in the passenger seat. "Fasten your seat belt," he told her as he closed the door.

"It's going to be a bumpy night." He heard her mutter the line from an old movie as he went around to the driver's side.

Marc might have laughed, but he was too strung out to allow any emotion through. Even with the blood he'd taken from her last night, he was still on the edge of being feral. Flight triggered pursuit. Although the ancient instinct was the first thing a young male was taught to control, the instinct never went away. If she ran again, he might bleed her dry this time. He was still fighting hard against the need to drag her beneath him and take her, blood or no blood. Catching her meant he'd won, and winning was an aphrodisiac.

He gave his head a hard shake. He had no time for this! He got in the Jeep and slammed the door, grateful for the small shade the interior provided. He hoped the Cherokee came equipped with air-conditioning.

Now, where to go? Having the SUV and the woman gave him a chance, but only a small one. They weren't going to stop coming for him— Gavin wasn't the kind who ever stopped.

He'd heard a plane in the sky around dawn, but they hadn't spotted him then. Luck couldn't be counted on to last. He badly needed a place to sleep, to eat, and to get the drugs out of his system; a place to lie low and recoup. But where?

He couldn't head home; that would put his Family stronghold in jeopardy.

Maybe there was a map in the duffel on her lap. Marcus reached across the seat and had to tug it away from her, because she was holding it in a death grip. Her nerves were as tightly strung as his, and he knew she was too afraid to be aware of what sang between them. He wished *he* could stuff the awareness down a hole in his conscience.

He undid all the many zippered compartments of the bag and combed through it. Since she'd had a spare set of car keys, there might be a spare weapon in the bag as well. He found only a few items of clothing, some cash, a Discman, a CD case, and her driver's license.

"Josephine Elliot," he read. She lived in Phoenix. She was twenty-seven and was five feet five inches tall. She certainly didn't match the weight listed on the license.

He flipped through the CD case and was disgusted with the music selection. Chick stuff like Alicia Keys and Norah Jones.

He looked at her chest. "I'd thought you'd have better taste, Josephine."

Jo realized he was talking about the rock band

logo on her shirt. "This was a present. Leave my stuff alone."

"I like road music. You have any rap? Hip-hop? And what are you doing with a cop gun like a Beretta?"

"It was a present," she said again.

"Your dad a cop?"

"Mother." She didn't know why she was telling him these personal things. "And my sister."

Her dad was a pilot, as was her brother. She'd always wanted to fly.

She'd flown, and then she'd fallen, and now here she was with a monster. No one expected her home for at least a week, and no one knew exactly where she'd gone. She didn't even have her cell phone with her. *Stupid, stupid, stupid.* What had she been thinking?

She hadn't been. She'd been hurting. She'd let the hurt take over her life, and look where it had gotten her.

Captured by a dangerous stranger, whom she was attuned to in a way she'd never experienced before. She supposed the hyperawareness was some sort of survival instinct.

Marc found a pair of wire-rimmed sunglasses on the visor. They didn't fit him very well, but they blocked the blistering desert light.

He also found a bottle of fancy "sports"

water in Josephine's bag. Though he'd drunk deeply from the woman the night before, he was still dehydrated, along with all his other problems.

He drank half the water, then tossed the bottle to Josephine. "You need liquids," he told her. "And plenty of sleep."

She unscrewed the lid and gulped down the other half of the bottle. Then she eyed him nervously. "Now what?"

"Sleep, Josephine." He used his dwindling reserves of energy to make the command a telepathic one that she couldn't help but obey.

Then Marc started the Jeep and drove back along the track she'd made to her campsite. Eventually he'd find a road. He'd decide which way to go when he got there.

Chapter Three

Jo lifted her head from the pillow and sniffed. "What's that?"

She knew what the aroma wafting through the small motel room was, but normally her stomach wouldn't have rumbled or her mouth begun to water as she caught a whiff of cooked meat.

Her captor closed the door and crossed the few steps to the bed, where he'd left her tied to the metal frame.

She had vague memories of the day, very vague. She'd dozed a lot, and he'd run the air-conditioning too high. There must have been a stop for gas. She'd heard his deep voice asking questions, though she had no recollection of anyone answering, no memory of any stranger's emotions intruding on her.

She'd lifted her head while they were stopped, intending to call for help. But he'd been beside her instantly. He held a bottle of cold water to her lips, and she drank greedily. And there'd been candy bars. She remembered salty peanuts and chocolate that she'd devoured with greedy lust at his urging. His voice was like chocolate, dark bittersweet whispering in her ear, or maybe inside her head, urging her to take care of herself while somehow making it sound like sin.

Now the aroma of greasy meat brought her fully back to consciousness. She looked around and found that she had some memory of being guided into this room by a hand on her arm.

It was a small, square cell of a place. The walls were a dull gray, the furniture sparse and shabby, and the double bed sagged in the middle. An air conditioner covered the room's only window. There was a door that led to a bathroom and the door to the outside. She had a feeling he was always going to be between her and the door to freedom.

"That's right," he said, and put two brown paper bags on the bedside table. He switched on the lamp, which gave more of a fitful glow than any real illumination, then squatted beside the bed and untied her.

He'd used strips from her shirt to restrain her. "I don't have that many clothes with me," she complained.

"This one was already ruined," he reminded her.

"I could have replaced the buttons."

It was silly to complain about something so unimportant as a piece of clothing, but it was easier than thinking about why the shirt had been destroyed.

A shudder of fear went through her. She wanted to ask how long he was going to hold her prisoner, why he was keeping her, what he was going to do.

She asked, "What's in the bags?"

"Hamburgers." He pulled the only chair over by the small table. It creaked when he sat on it. He took one of the burgers out of the bag and handed it to her.

The wrapped bundle was warm and heavy in her hand. The fragrance made her mouth water. The look she turned on him was accusatory. "I'm a vegetarian."

"Not anymore."

She wanted to refuse to eat, but why be a hypocrite? She wanted it. She wolfed it down in three large bites, then licked mustard and ketchup off her lips. She held out her hand, and he put a second burger into it. She didn't make such a quick job of this one, but settled back against the headboard with the thin pillows at her back and her legs folded beneath her, and savored. He handed her a small carton of orange juice, and that was delicious, too.

Marc settled his big frame as comfortably as he could on the wooden chair and watched Josephine. The food he'd brought her wasn't anything fancy, yet she took absolute, sensual pleasure out of it. She took these moments to forget he was there, to forget her fear and simply enjoy what she had.

She was living in the moment, and that was a good thing. She hadn't been doing that when he'd found her. She'd been living in the past, and in pain.

He ate two of the burgers he'd brought, but they only satisfied a small part of his need. He was hungry for her, but it wouldn't be safe for her if he indulged that hunger so soon. The mark he'd left on her throat hadn't healed yet, a sure sign he'd taken too much too quickly.

It still amazed him that she'd been there for him. All her psychic senses had been wide-open, waiting— calling. Though this mortal woman didn't know the psychic connection her soul craved, he recognized his future mate, even maddened by thirst.

He'd never believed in fate and legends, or even the ancient moon goddess the Families revered, but old Selene had come through for him in his darkest hour. Now it was up to him to make the most of the miracle and protect what the goddess had given him. As much as he could. His own freedom had to come first.

"How are you feeling?" he asked, gently probing the edges of her mind.

"Where are we?" she asked.

He sensed that she was still hungry and passed her a third hamburger. "There's milk." She held out a hand, and he twisted off the cap of the plastic bottle before handing it to her.

"You haven't answered me," Josephine said after she drained the milk.

"Eat," he suggested.

"We're in a motel." She looked around, with more attention than when he'd come in. "How? Where?"

"There's no phone. No one knows you're here."

He'd paid cash for two nights, and had been as hypnotically persuasive with the run-down motel's owner as the drugs in him and his weakness allowed, telling the old man to forget about him, to ignore the man in room two. He'd been equally persuasive with the counterman at the greasy spoon across the dusty road that ran through this tiny excuse for a town.

She brought an annoyed gaze back to him. "What's your name?"

"Cage," he answered.

He got a skeptically raised eyebrow at this. He knew it sounded dramatic, but vampire culture was like that.

"Really. Marc Cage."

Marcus Cage of Family Caeg, to be formal about it. Someday the knowledge might mean something to her, but this was no time to consider possible futures. Always live in the moment when in trouble, concentrate on getting out.

She wished she hadn't asked, didn't know why she had. Putting a name to the brute humanized him somewhat. Which might not be a smart move. She didn't want to think of Cage as a person. He was her kidnapper. She had to keep emotional distance. She didn't want to worry about what he was feeling and thinking, other than as it applied to her survival.

There were some basic things she needed to know: *Are you going to kill me? Are you going to rape me?*

"What now?" she asked.

"You want more to eat?" When she shook her head, he got up, and said, "Come on."

He took her arm again once she was on her feet. She hoped they were going outside; maybe she'd get a chance to shout for help. Instead, he took her to the bathroom.

"Ladies first," he said, and pushed her before him into the room.

Jo looked at the toilet, then back to where he stood blocking the doorway. "I don't use that with anyone watching."

"I won't watch." He turned his back to her. "I'll even close my eyes."

"You could wait outside."

He didn't answer, just stood there filling the narrow doorway like a statue carved out of dark marble. After a few moments she gave in to the call of nature. While she did, he stripped off his clothes. She tried not to look, but by the time she was done, her view was of his naked backside.

Every muscle was so beautifully sculpted, Michelangelo could have signed the work. His skin was as smooth as marble, perfectly proportioned from wide shoulders to narrow waist and down to the curve of his ass and hard-muscled thighs and calves. He had no scars, she noted. There was not a mole or freckle on him.

"Done?" he asked.

"Yes." She stood and backed into the farthest corner of the small bathroom.

"I'm turning around now," he told her.

She gasped.

He chuckled. "Don't stare. It's rude."

When he moved, she closed her eyes. That was no protection, of course. Pretending this juggernaut of a man wasn't there was stupid. He was standing next to her in only a couple of steps. She was aware of his presence like a shadow passing across the sun. Only instead of being cooler, she grew warm.

His hands touched her hips, then skimmed up her waist. She pressed herself back against the wall, wedged between the sink and toilet. There was nowhere for her to go, and his hands were on her. Her head spun, and her body went heavy and hot in a way that was totally unexpected and unwanted. It took her a moment to realize that he'd taken off her shirt, and that she'd lifted her arms to help him do it. What was the matter with her?

Marc wasn't surprised when Josephine's eyes flew open, and the dreamy expression that briefly crossed her face disappeared in a burst of panic. Her reaction shook him enough to make him remember the reason they were in the room. He stepped back and turned to the shower. "You want to go first?" he asked, and turned on the water.

Jo abandoned modesty as soon as water began spraying out of the showerhead. She took off the rest of her clothes and squeezed past the naked man into the stall. He passed her a sliver of soap and closed the thin plastic curtain. She made the most of the sudden privacy to quickly wash off days' worth of grime. She worked the soap into a pitiful lather and scrubbed at her hair and skin. It was surprising how quickly basic things like food and cleanliness came to feel like the ultimate in luxury.

"Save some for me," she heard Cage say.

"No," she called back over the sound of the water.

"Then we'll have to share."

She knew it was a mistake even to try to tease this man when the shower curtain was shoved aside a moment later.

Marc slid his big body into the small space. Cramped as it was, he almost felt like he'd died and gone to heaven as water washed over him, and the scent of Josephine's skin, warm from the water, sleek and slippery with soap, was crushed against his chest and thighs. He grew hard instantly. His erection pressed against her. He put his arms around her, having to move slowly and carefully in the confined space. He stood for a long time, holding her, letting the water work on tired muscles, waiting, hoping she would relax.

After a while he began to touch her. He had

to move very slowly in the tight space, but the gentleness helped her. He needed her to get used to his touch. He wanted her craving it, and perhaps that would come in time. If they were to bond, it was necessary for desire to grow between them.

He glided his hands up and down her back, over her lovely, rounded buttocks, over her hips and up to her waist. He sleeked his hands down her thighs, then came up to rub his fingers through her hair, massaging her scalp.

Her head moved against his hands, and the small sound she made was one of pleasure at last. The fear was still inside her, quivering in her belly, beating in her heart, roaring in her head, but her skin enjoyed his touch.

Her head fell back, her face full in the stream of water. He kissed her then, his mouth covering hers as the water beat against his back. He was all too aware of her breasts pressed against his chest, of her taste, of the clean scent of her skin. She opened her lips for him.

Though she stayed still in his embrace, a fear-driven spike of adrenaline shot through her. She wasn't ready for this.

Besides, more than her body, he still needed her blood, and couldn't spare giving her his. She wasn't ready for that yet, either.

This was no time for him to think about a bonding courtship.

He lifted his head and turned off the water. "Time for bed," he told her. He snatched thin white towels from the shelf over the toilet and handed her a couple.

Jo shook as she dried herself off. She was so weak she could barely stand, so confused she couldn't think, so aroused she could hardly bear the shame. Her head was spinning, and she couldn't feel what he was feeling. Maybe because she was feeling too much herself? Maybe because he could shut himself off from her? She should be glad of that, yet it made her feel lonely. She was used to reading emotions. Now she had to do it the hard way, and she looked at him.

What she saw was a man weary to the point of collapse. Her heart went out to him, though sympathy for the devil was stupid.

It made her even more confused when the devil picked her up and carried her to the bed cradled in his arms like a baby. She couldn't manage to protest, not even when he turned off the dim light and lay down beside her. The sagging mattress made sure that they rolled together.

For a long time she was acutely aware of her

back pressed to his front, the animal warmth they shared, his arm across her body, holding her prisoner yet somehow comforting. She was aware when his breathing shifted from wakefulness to sleep. She counted those slow breaths like another person might count sheep. Eventually she drifted off, too.

Chapter Four

Doors. Where had all the doors come from? Endless corridor of doors. Each one locked, with little barred windows. People could look in, but no one could get out. Everything was white. Cold, frozen white. No fire outside, only on the inside. He burned—pain, fever. Fear? Nofearno-fearnofear. Don't give them fear.

Fear. There was nothing but fear, and the ground and the sky changing places over and over. Screaming metal, screaming wind. Scream-ing inside, silent outside. It would be so easy to scream, impossible to stop. No time to scream. Her hands working, eyes working, voice calm. Training. All training. A puppet going through the motions. Trying to live, waiting for death.

*   *   *

Death was part of the plan. Had to be. Cold, calculated, step-by-step torture leading down to the door marked Death. Endless nights and days of torture. Needles filled with fire. Needles filled with ice. Fading in and out—pain that came with sleep, pain that came with waking. And hunger. Always the growing hunger leading to weakness, madness, murderous need.

As the needle slid into her arm she looked into the stranger's face. It was cold, hard; the only expression in the eyes was one of faint curiosity. A merciless man in a merciless place. She was a lab animal laid out on a cold metal slab. Restraints held her down. Her skin was freezing cold. Everything was white, walls, ceiling, floor. Gleaming metal monitoring machines reflected the whiteness. There was a door in the distance, behind the torturer's head. She had to get to that door, to all the doors beyond that door. She had to get out.

"You're going to kill me."

Her voice was not her own, but deep and male. Her skin was not her own, but her mind filled the muscular body, and her mind wanted answers.

There was no answer. They never talked to her.

Then the reaction to the injection kicked in, and the world turned to fire.

He couldn't make his hands work. They didn't look like his hands, they were soft and small, and shaking. There were controls in front of him he didn't know how to use, even if he could stop the shaking. His gaze riveted on lights flashing ominously red, and data he had no idea how to read. Fear clawed at him, and the guilt was beyond bearing.

He was going to die. Worse, others were going to die because of him.

Through the cockpit window he saw the mountain rushing toward him. Rushing, but in slow motion. Everything happened far too fast, and far too slowly at the same time. It made him dizzy. His head began to spin, and the plane began to spin, auguring in toward the ground.

No one to blame but himself.

Falling. Falling.

Marc flinched hard as his soul crashed back into his body. It brought him half-out of the bed, and off the woman tucked half-beneath him. He wiped a sweaty hand across his face— fear sweat, he hated to admit. His heart rate had kicked up, pounding close to human normal as the dream still half filled his head. He sat up, placing his bare feet on the rough, worn carpet.

He looked at his hands, flexing fingers that were large and competent. In the dream they had been numb and useless. *He'd* been useless.

At least he hadn't hit the ground. He'd heard somewhere that if you dreamed of falling and hit, you died in your sleep. Of course if that were true, how would anyone who'd actually finished the fall convey the information back to Urban Legend Central?

The thoughts made him smile, almost made him feel normal. It reminded him that there had been a time when he'd been more than a creature pared down to fixation on his continued existence. There'd been a time when Marc Cage wasn't an abusive jerk.

New nightmare images rushed in, dizzying, devastating, and he realized suddenly that the nightmare was not his. He turned to Josephine, who was caught in a nightmare of her own. He touched her shoulder and discovered muscles stiff as stone. Through the physical contact, he felt what was going through her subconscious.

The white room. Cold. Fire. The watcher.

She was curled in a frozen ball of pain and

fear that didn't belong to her, any more than his nightmare had belonged to him.

"Josephine." He spoke her name out loud, then in her mind. *Josephine.*

The sound was like an alarm far away, beyond the doors, beyond the impassive observer's face, beyond . . .

Come back to me, Josephine.

Not a sound. It was a name.

Josephine.

Hers.

She blinked, and the restraints faded. The face faded. The room faded.

The pain—

Jo woke with a soundless scream. Her eyes flew open to—

"It was a dream."

The rich, deep voice wasn't hers—but she had sounded like that. In the—

"It *wasn't* a dream." She turned a glare on Cage. "Those were memories. What the hell happened to you?"

"You had a dream. A bad dream. That's all."

He put his big hands on her shoulders, and she felt engulfed by them. His presence was overwhelming, more than just physically. He caught her gaze and held it. There was a lot of power in the depths of his deep, dark eyes.

"It was a nightmare."

He *wanted* her to believe it.

The memories of the white room and torture were clear and crisp and horrible, but she went along with his wishes and nodded. She couldn't bear to do anything else at the moment.

"You had a dream about a plane crash," he said.

That wasn't what she'd dreamed at all. Had *he* dreamed about the crash? Was that possible? It seemed like he could read her mind and bring her comfort if she'd let him. Maybe it was possible—no. She shook her head.

"You're a pilot, aren't you? And the crash happened. That's what left your psychic senses open and screaming when I found you."

"I wasn't screaming until *after* we met."

"I heard you."

She found herself looking at his chest rather than his face. She would not look into those eyes. She would not let him pull her life out of her. He had no right.

But—what had *he* been through?

It didn't matter, she told herself. And it *must* have been a dream, as he said—psychic senses—what the hell was he talking about? The head injury had just messed up her head.

"Being around people hurt." She hated that

she admitted that much, but he was the only one who seemed to understand.

"Survivor's guilt," he said. "That's what made you so vulnerable. It's not safe to be alone out in that desert. People disappear out there every year and are never heard from again. You weren't consciously looking for trouble when you found it, but you were waiting. You didn't have your gun nearby—"

"You said it wouldn't have done any good."

"With anyone but me, it would have." He shook her gently, like reprimanding a child. "There are easier ways of committing suicide, Josephine."

"I don't want to kill myself!"

"But you're guilty about being alive."

His words stung like ice water in her face. "This is none of your business, Cage."

She was fully awake now, all the dreams and memories shoved in the back of the mind where they belonged. She was also aware that they were two naked people on a bed, bodies touching, emotions running high.

"Wrong."

That was all he said, one simple, adamant word. A word that unequivocally stated that everything about her was his. Absolutely everything.

"Oh, good lord." Tears sprang to her eyes, and she wasn't quite sure why. She wasn't exactly afraid. Something inside her sizzled, but it wasn't exactly anger.

His arms slipped off her shoulders and came around her. He pulled her close and just held her. Her head rested on his shoulders, and the tears came. She tasted salt on her lips and felt the moisture on his skin, where her cheek rested against him.

"You shouldn't cry," his bass voice rumbled in her ear. "You're already dehydrated."

She sniffled and lifted her head off his shoulder. "Bite me."

He didn't take this as the insult it was intended to be. "Later," he told her.

She wondered what time it was, how long they'd been sleeping, how long they'd been awake. The room was dim and cool, like a cave they'd run to to hide from the world, a place to lick their wounds and recover strength. There was danger all around. She sensed it from Cage.

She'd never been *so* aware of anyone in her life—mentally, psychically, physically.

He was being hunted, and she, as a hostage, was his ticket to freedom. She had to remember that she meant nothing to him besides his own selfish ends.

Her emotions danced like static electricity through all Marc's senses. His Josephine was a confused whirlwind of feelings. He shouldn't have comforted her or confronted her. But she needed both, even if she didn't want it; even if giving it and drawing her closer to him endangered them both.

Even worse, he'd made claims and staked territory, and she knew it. Stupid Prime instinct. It wasn't good for a species when the mating drive kept trying to override the need for survival. Or maybe it was the need to bond that overwhelmed every sensible instinct in a psychic species.

He was an idiot. Worse, he was thirsty, and his control was slipping. He wasn't all that noble, or much of a gentleman. Her naked body was pressed close to his, and the feel of her was exciting him more by the moment. It wasn't only blood he craved. It had been a long time since he'd had a woman. It had been a long time since he'd had any contact that didn't bring pain and humiliation. There were a lot of bad memories he needed to wipe away. Like any Prime, he needed to establish dominance and control in every possible way.

And it would be so good to share pleasure once more.

He ran a hand down the length of her relaxed spine, appreciating her soft, supple skin. Her head came up off his shoulder again and she was suddenly stiff, faintly trembling with a surge of fear.

All right. He knew how to make love. He could make her want him, if he started slowly and gently and used everything he knew from decades as a sexually active Prime to get her so keyed up, she'd beg him to take what he wanted. It would only be a matter of slow, deliberate, delicious coercion, arousing her flesh so thoroughly that it would override any objections her mind could bring up.

Or he could bite her. When a Prime drew blood from a partner, he gave pleasure in exchange. It was a fair price for life-giving sustenance, but she'd already been roughly overwhelmed by that kind of pleasure once; it had nearly been too much for her bruised mind. So much so that she probably didn't remember exactly what had happened out in the desert night. If he drank from her now, he was in control enough to give her the time of her life. He could sate her body, satisfy his blood thirst, then have her in as many ways and as many times as he wanted. That kind of sex would make up for a lot of privation.

She was a helpless prisoner, and he was totally in control. She couldn't stop him.

Marc let her go and scrambled to his feet. He turned his back on the woman and rubbed his hands across his face. He knew too well what it felt like to be helpless and at his captors' mercy. Not that they'd had any.

He was shaking when he turned back to her. She was kneeling on the bed, back arched, hands fisted at her sides, her face turned up to look at him. He couldn't keep from devouring her with his eyes, and those eyes saw beneath sweet female flesh to the tracery of vital life beneath the skin. He could sense her body heat, smell the mingled scents that made the unique perfume that was her. Combined with all that was the vibrant swirl of her emotions.

He was hard and shaking with need.

"You have no idea how you look to me, do you?" His deep voice was rough with his need.

She met his gaze, blinked. "Your eyes are glowing."

"Yeah. That happens."

Her gaze slid down the length of his body. "Are you going to rape me?"

Her frank stare almost made him want to cover his erection. He concentrated very hard on calming down and managed the faintest of gestures. "I'm not," he answered.

"Right now?"

He shook his head. "Not ever."

She slid cautiously toward the end of the bed and brought up the worn bedspread to cover herself. "Never?" she persisted. "Can I trust you not to touch me?"

"No," he admitted. He was no saint, or a chivalrous Clan boy who'd die before dishonoring their chosen lady. "But I'm not going to touch you right now. That's all you can count on. We don't need the complication."

He didn't give her much to go on, but Jo found Cage's honesty reassuring. She watched, wrapped in the bedding, while he turned away and put on his ragged trousers. Muscular as he was, he still moved with compact grace that was hard not to appreciate.

Had his eyes really been glowing? There was so much about him that was strange. "Didn't you have a sunburn yesterday?" she asked as he walked toward the bathroom.

"I'm a fast healer. Come on," he added. He gestured for her to follow. "I need your help."

She didn't want to be confined with him in there again, but didn't suppose there was any getting out of it. She rose to her feet and wrapped the bedspread around her like a sarong. It wound around her slender body a surprising number of times, which somehow made her feel safer, though it weighed her down when she moved.

He waited at the doorway to gesture her in before him. "Help you do what?" she asked as she moved past him.

"Shave," he answered. "Maybe you'll even get lucky and cut me."

Chapter Five

"Why do you want to shave your head?" Jo asked.

His hair was already quite short. It was curly and black, and currently covered with a lather he'd managed to work up from the thin bar of soap. The blue plastic razor in her hand was from the few toiletries in her bag.

She turned the razor over and over in her fingers. It would make a pitiful weapon, which was probably why he was letting her hold it. And when had she started thinking about everyday objects as weapons?

Was acquaintance with Cage turning her into a survivor, or a barbarian?

"Change is good," he said.

For a moment she thought he was answering her thought, then she remembered that she'd asked him about why he wanted to get rid of his hair.

"Is this really a fashion statement?" she asked suspiciously. "Or are you trying to look different than the face on the wanted posters?"

"Clever girl." Seated on the toilet, he reached over her to turn on the tap, then leaned over the sink. "Do this before the soap dries."

Well, how hard could it be? Jo made a careful pass with the razor across Cage's head.

"Ow."

"Sorry." She didn't know why she apologized—automatic politeness? Then again, why antagonize her captor?

"Am I bleeding?"

Then again, why not? "Do you want to be?"

He chuckled, and the deep, rich sound filled the tiny room. He turned his head to look at her. "Do you want a taste?"

The question sent a shiver through her, and the oddest momentary sensation—like a craving—through her.

"You're sick, Cage."

He didn't answer, but turned his head so she could get back to work.

To really see what she was doing, she had to lean over Cage's big body, putting a hand on his shoulder to steady herself. Disconcerting as the closeness was, there was something almost comforting in the pattern of drawing the razor across his skin, rinsing it in the running water, then moving on. Her work progressed slowly, but Cage was patient. She rather liked the sound the razor made scraping off his short, thick hair. Every now and then her breasts brushed his back or her thigh touched his side, and the contact sent little shock waves through her.

She was relieved to take a step back, and announce, "Done."

Cage splashed water over his head to get off the remaining soap. Then he stood to look into the mirror over the sink. "Not bad. Reminds me of my days in the Marines."

He took the razor from her and made a quick job of shaving his face.

She barely recognized him when he finished. She preferred men with hair, which gave her another reason for disliking him. Yet the lack of hair somehow emphasized his strong cheekbones and throat, made his dark eyes seem larger, and made his large, sensual mouth the focus of his face.

All she could say was, "You were a Marine?"

"Back in the day." He smoothed a hand over his freshly shaved head. "You do good work."

He rubbed the dark sprinkling of hair on his chest. "You do body waxing?"

She gestured around the dingy little bathroom. "We offer a full line of treatments at the Grubby Acres Resort. Aromatherapy, massage, and facials available. Would you care to see a price list, sir?"

"I'd rather have something to eat."

The mention of food made her stomach rumble. She was so hungry all of a sudden that it made her wonder how long it had been since their last meal. How long had they been asleep? Was it day or night? There were no windows in the bathroom, and the small bedroom window was filled by the noisy air conditioner. The low-wattage lightbulb in the bedroom's only lamp gave a feeling of perpetual twilight. How long was he going to keep her here, hidden from daylight?

Claustrophobia gripped her worse than physical hunger, but a few deep breaths calmed her. By the time she had herself under control, he'd moved into the bedroom. Jo followed, with the bottom of the bedspread held in her hand to make it easier to walk.

Cage's back was to her, and she saw that he was counting out bills from the cash he'd taken from her. With his attention diverted, she swiftly unwrapped the cloth from her body and tossed it over his head.

She managed to make it to the door while he threw off the cloth; she grabbed the knob and had it open . . . then he tackled her.

She heard the door slam as she hit the floor hard. The impact knocked the breath out of her, keeping her from howling in angry frustration. Though fighting the big man was impossible, she hit him on the shoulder.

"Let me *go*," she said when she got her breath back. "Just let me go!"

"No."

Marc probably understood her need for freedom better than Josephine did. He admired that she'd managed to surprise him, even as he was annoyed that he'd relaxed enough to let that happen. He needed her for cover to keep himself alive.

He also needed Josephine the way a Prime needed the woman meant to share the mating bond with him. He was already attached to her, body and soul. His prayer had been answered, which was a miracle, and a mistake. His side of the bond was only going to get deeper as he fed, and as their minds and personalities meshed.

She was rightly frightened of him, rightly furious, and she hadn't tasted him yet. Those would all help her fight her attraction to him, and lack of bonding on her part would come in handy if he had to abandon her.

He had to protect his Family; he had to protect the secrets of his world. He couldn't let caring for Josephine put him in danger. He wouldn't willingly walk away from her if he could help it; but if he had to abandon her to survive, he would.

Right now, he didn't want to walk away. He had a naked woman beneath him, and he was fiercely aware of every inch of her, of every curve, every muscle. Her scent fueled his thirst for her.

But this was no time for him to get a hard-on again—not so soon after he'd promised not to touch her right now.

He gave his head a hard shake. Then he got up, scooped her off the floor, and carried her back to the bed. He found the rags of her shirt he'd used before and tied her hands to the bedframe. This time he added a gag. The look of hatred she gave him shot straight through him. He tossed the bedspread across her before he left. The last thing he wanted to see was a naked woman waiting on the bed when he walked back into the room.

Why tempt himself if he didn't have to?

* * *

"You don't have to sulk; I know you're hungry."

"I am not sulking," Jo informed Cage. He was sitting on the chair, she was perched on the edge of the bed, and the nightstand, piled with food, was between them. The aroma of the fried chicken was making her mouth water.

"Try it, you'll like it."

His deep voice was almost as persuasive as the smell. She put her hand up as he tried to pass the paper plate with a piece of fried chicken on it to her. "I told you before that I'm a vegetarian."

She rubbed her wrists, which were bruised from trying to work off the strips of cloth that had bound her. No luck there. The first thing he'd done when he returned was untie her and let her get dressed. He'd changed, too, out of his torn and dirty sleeveless T-shirt into a clean white cotton one. He'd taken the shirt out of a package that he'd brought back with the food. The shirt was a little tight on him and outlined the ripped muscles of his arms and chest.

"This is all I could find to wear," he said, when he noticed her looking at his shirt. "The gas station has a few supplies, not much." He gestured toward a plastic bag he'd left near the door. "I got you some shampoo."

She refused to show the gratitude that she felt.

After all, if he hadn't driven off before she could pack up her tent, she'd have all of her toiletries with her.

He handed her a cola, and she gulped it down. "Thanks. The gag made my mouth dry."

She didn't expect him to look guilty, and he didn't. "Eat," he urged. "You need protein."

He'd brought a bag of fried chicken, corn on the cob, fried potatoes, rolls and butter, along with milk and sodas. She wanted it all, but she eyed him suspiciously. "Why do I think you're trying to fatten me up?"

He looked her up and down, assessing her in a critical way. "You need more exercise. A cardio routine, weights, yoga for flexibility."

"Don't tell me; in your real life you're a personal trainer?"

He gave a slight shrug. "Gym rat. Working out's good for you."

"I've just finished six weeks of physical therapy, thank you very much. I don't want—" She snapped her mouth shut.

Her life was none of his business. His life was none of hers. She wished it didn't interest her. Since he was all she had to focus on, it was natural to latch on to any information she found out about him. Information might help her find a way to escape. So far, she knew he was an ex-

Marine and into working out. That made him a fit, trained soldier—points in his favor, not hers.

There were other things about him that she couldn't comprehend, but they were also not in her favor.

"Eat the chicken," he urged. "You know you want to."

"It's cruel to eat animals."

"Not chicken. They deserve what happens to them."

"How can you say that?"

He laughed at her outrage. He ripped quickly through a drumstick, then said, "My great-grandmother has a farm in upstate New York. Most of my family are city mice, but I used to spend summers in the country when I was a kid. You know anything about the butter-and-egg business?"

"Yes," she answered, and watched his strongly arched eyebrows go up in surprise.

He bit into a chicken breast, then went on. "I got to know her chickens really well. Meanest bastards you ever met. They'll chase you and peck you. And they're really stupid, as well as bad-tempered. Trust me, chickens are not our friends. Chickens are food." He finished off the breast and picked up another chicken leg.

Jo'd been watching him the whole time he'd

been eating, and talking, and eating. She couldn't take it anymore. "Give me that."

He let out a deep, rumbling laugh when she snatched the meat out of his hand.

He put another piece on her plate, along with corn and potatoes. "I told you you were hungry."

She hated that he was right—and that the meat was really, really good.

Chapter Six

Jo turned on the shower and thought back to what Cage had said. He'd used the words *my great-grandmother has*.

Has. Not past tense.

So, his great-grandmother must be a really old woman. And he'd mentioned the butter-and-egg business.

Her own great-grandfather had gotten out of that profession back in the mid-1940s and moved the family from New York to Arizona. He'd seen the end coming of what had been a flourishing nineteenth- and early-twentieth-century way of life. She'd heard stories about it when she'd visited him in a retirement home when she was little. The old-time industry, with individual companies brokering eggs and butter from small farms and reselling them, had been driven out of existence by super-market chains and factory farms by the 1950s.

And something in the way Cage spoke about the butter-and-egg business made it sound like he'd been a kid back when his great-grandmother sold her eggs to the butter-and-egg brokers.

That was impossible, of course, because Cage could be no more than in his early thirties.

He had to be messing with her head, taking psychological advantage of her. And feeding her up for something, she just knew it.

At least I'll be clean when the apocalypse comes.

And at least she wasn't sharing the small stall with the oversized Cage.

Even when he wasn't coercing, the man was *influencing* her. She didn't know how he did it. She supposed it was because her world had been reduced to him and the hotel room, where there was only the lamp for light, and the drone of the air conditioner blocked off all other sound. The room didn't even have a clock, and she didn't know where her watch had gotten to. There had to be other people around, but oddly, she couldn't sense any but Cage's presence.

Jo turned off the shower with an angry twist and grabbed a towel. Hiding in the bathroom wasn't going to help. She got dressed and marched into the bedroom while her anger was strong enough to make her brave.

Cage looked up from reading a newspaper, and asked, "Were you really going to run out of here buck naked?"

"Of course."

"I'm shocked." He regarded her carefully in her shorts and black T-shirt with a large white X splashed across the front. "I really am." He shook his head. "Women these days."

She got the feeling he was quite serious. "Spend much time in a hospital, and you lose any self-consciousness." Which was none of his business. "I want out," she announced. "You have to let me go."

He tilted one arched eyebrow. "We aren't going to have the 'you haven't got any right to be doing this' conversation, are we?" He folded the paper and gave her his full, serious attention. "Of course I don't have any right to do this. I'm not a sociopath. Sociopaths believe they can do anything they want, simply because they can."

"But—"

"I'm not a nice man," he continued, "but I do know right from wrong."

"But if you know this is wrong—"

"I suffer guilt and anxiety, but I can live with it."

He was teasing her. He looked serious, he spoke with calm earnestness, but he was teasing her. She could feel it. She could feel him, read him, at least a little.

Of course, he didn't want her to be afraid of him. That was what this was about—he was trying to keep her off-balance. He could control her easier if she—

Oh, for God's sake, the man was huge! And faster than any mortal had a right to be. He didn't have to play psychological games to control her. When she'd tried to escape an hour ago he'd stopped her, but had he tied her up or beaten her? No. He'd tossed her the shampoo and told her she needed something to occupy her.

So he *was* just teasing her. Though he was also telling her the truth. She didn't understand why, but—

"I know," he said. "Try not to think so hard. It'll give you a headache." He picked up the newspaper and handed her a couple of sections. "Try the comics," he suggested.

The paper was a copy of the *Republic*. The date could have been today's or a couple of days ago. She'd had two meals and a couple of showers, but that didn't give her any real indication of the amount of time Cage had been holding her.

"Where'd you get this?" she asked him.

"Stole it out of the back of a car."

"You get to have all the fun."

"Yep."

"Where is here?" she asked him.

"Don't know."

She hated his getting all terse on her. "I'm ready to start clawing at the walls, Cage."

He gave her another raised-eyebrow glance, and his expression made her blush. "If you want something to claw, sweetheart . . ."

His voice was deep, dark, and suggestive of sin.

She perched primly on the side of the sagging bed, her feet firmly on the floor, and made herself read the front page. There was a story about wildfires in several spots across the state; it was suspected that the fires were arson. She didn't understand why anyone would purposefully start a fire that could ravage a countryside and endanger people. She put down the paper.

"Are the fires near here?" she asked, unable not to worry about them. And to be reminded of her real life. She wondered if her brother was flying a plane for the Bureau of Land Management overhead right now.

"I don't know." He was reading the sports section.

Jo got up and paced the room. "You should find out. It could be important."

"I'll do that."

His laconic routine was infuriating her. Ordinarily she didn't have much of a temper. She had never raised her hand in anger. She didn't get into shouting matches or emotional scenes. But Cage brought out very strong emotions in her.

"I'd *love* to throw something at you right now," she told him.

"You could."

Marc wished she would. She had no idea what she was doing to him, how the craving was growing. The faint soap on her clean skin didn't disguise her female scent, which nearly drove him over the edge with desire. The way she moved like a hunted animal brought all his predatory instincts to the surface. And he was getting very, very thirsty.

What was the matter with him? The source of all he needed was only a few feet away; all he had to do was reach out and take her. Instead, he sat burning up, a newspaper covering the evidence of how hard he was.

Go ahead, he prayed. *Throw something. Give me an excuse to pounce.*

Normally, he'd simply seduce a partner and bring them mutual satisfaction, then say goodbye the next morning. But that wasn't an option. There was only one road for them to go down, but he didn't know how to start on it. Maybe a month from now—if he could get them out of this alive.

Cage's deep voice penetrated Jo down to her marrow, and something in her soul responded to the call. The next thing she knew she was standing in front of him, shaking like a leaf, but not wanting to run away.

She found enough courage to look him in the eye, and ask, "Was that terror or telepathy, Cage?"

Marc had enough control left to smile. "That's Sergeant Cage."

He put his arm around her shoulder and pulled her to sit beside him on the bed. The old springs sagged inward, making them lean back. The bed was trying to make them lie down; why not go with it?

Her body heat sent aching need through him. Her heartbeat pounded inside his head. Her blood and her being called and called . . .

He couldn't resist rubbing his cheek against her soft blond hair, still damp, fragrant, seductive. Everything about her was seductive. Need curled tightly around him, in him, from her, for her. He fought to keep from stroking her skin, from caressing her breasts. He wanted to arouse her as much as he was aroused.

He didn't know why he resisted his impulses; maybe he was too used to ordinary dates. He wanted her body as much as he needed her blood. He could take it, and would if he must, but if he could have her heart and mind as well . . .

"Listen to me, Josephine. Listen to me."

"What do you want?"

"I'm thirsty. You have to understand what I need." His fangs were growing. The fight not to extend them was so hard, he could barely get out the words. His thoughts reached out when the words failed.

Fire.

She was suddenly burning up from the inside.

I'm on fire.

The fire was inside him, driving him mad, killing him.

He needed her help, was begging for it. How could she refuse anyone in that much pain? His pain blinded her, deafened her. All that was left was her sense of touch. She was aware of hard, tense muscles, of his arm around her, and the solid wall of his chest.

Help.

She didn't know what she could do, but her hand came up to touch his face. She stroked his cheek. His flesh was hot with fever.

His hand grasped her wrist and brought it to his mouth. Soft lips and warm breath brushed across her skin. Pain sharper than needles followed the kiss. Then she was filled with brightness, and bliss flooded her, consuming her until everything went dark.

Chapter Seven

He had given her pleasure, and he hadn't taken too much blood. Though she'd fainted, her life wasn't threatened. He'd been in control of his desire, and hadn't had sex with her even though he was still hard.

Chivalry hurt like hell. His balls were about to fall off, and here he was stretched out beside a sleeping woman, totally aroused and knowing he wasn't going to do a thing about it.

Well . . . "Never trust anyone completely, even yourself," he murmured, and slipped his hand under her shirt to cop a feel of her firm, round breasts. Nice breasts; small, but very nice. He touched a nipple with the tip of his forefinger and enjoyed the way it stirred and stiffened. When he touched her other nipple, she let out a soft moan that sent a shiver of lust through him.

He reluctantly pulled his hand back. She wasn't conscious; it wasn't fair.

He could feel her blood coursing through him, healing him. He was regaining strength, regaining his powers. He should be sleeping, letting the fresh blood work its magic while he slept.

Maybe he was too horny to sleep. And, strangely, he enjoyed watching Josephine sleep. There was no fear in her face right now, no tenseness in her muscles. She looked boneless as a sleeping cat, with her head turned to the side on the thin pillow, one hand at her side, the other arm stretched out across the mattress.

Studying her, he became aware of her scars for the first time. Straight lines of scarring with little dots of stitch marks on her left knee and right leg, burn scars on her left arm. He suspected he'd find more scars under her clothing. She'd mentioned being in the hospital, and physical therapy. He remembered living through the nightmare of her plane crash. She'd had a rough time recently, and now he was happening to her.

Well, life wasn't fair. And her scars would start healing as soon as she tasted his blood. At least he could make her physically whole once more, another fair exchange.

Marc rolled onto his back and worked on relaxing. It didn't help that Josephine turned onto her side and fitted her body against him, her head on his shoulder. It pleased him, even as he wondered if he could use this unconscious trust.

Tender and treacherous, that's me. But he had to be alert to any opportunity that might help him stay alive and free.

After a while, though, the comfort of Josephine's presence lulled him into healing sleep.

"Take her."

The voice whispered in his ear like the buzz of a mosquito, and made him shake his head. "What?"

"You know you want to."

Of course he wanted her. "Yes." He opened his eyes and looked around. White. Everywhere white. Familiar, imprisoning white. "No!"

"It was all a dream. Welcome home. Take her."

He knew that voice. The devil's own voice. The voice of the torturer turned seducer.

"Make her yours. Body and soul. Take what you want. Give her what she needs. Make her need."

Josephine lay on the cot in his white cage, naked, spread out like a feast. Her eyes were open, on him, full of fear, and he found the fear delicious. Her heartbeat raced like a frightened rabbit's. The frantic rhythm filled his senses.

"Blood need sings inside you. Take what you need. Everything you need."

Everything was a hell of a lot. He was Prime, and no Prime claimed a mate in only one way. The merging had to be total: fangs into flesh, thoughts blending, blood mingling, bodies thrusting and straining, completing—

"Inside her, in every way. Your blood in her, your cock in her. Do it."

Why not? It was what he wanted, all of him inside all of her. He ached as only a Prime could with wanting all of her.

He knelt between her outstretched legs, and slowly slid up the inside of her thighs. Her skin was soft velvet. His fingers moved against her, stroked warm, yielding flesh. He leaned forward, ready to guide himself into her, glanced up, and met her gaze.

She said, "I'm sharing this dream, you know."

Then someone knocked on the cell door.

The knock came again, harder and louder.

The sound brought Marc to his feet, waking as he hit the floor. His first thought was that she'd said "dream"—not "nightmare."

Then the knock sounded again, and he was instantly across the room. He put his ear to the door, and opened his senses. He didn't recognize the heartbeat or the scent of the man outside.

"Anyone in there?" a stranger's voice called. "Highway Patrol."

Marc swore silently, and opened the door to face a stout, uniformed man. At least it was dark outside, and he wasn't weak and drug-addled anymore. He was prepared to do whatever he had to do.

"Yes?" he asked.

"Sorry to wake you." The patrolman gestured toward the Jeep parked in front of the motel room door. "I thought the place was completely evacuated. Didn't the owner warn you about the fire before he left?"

Marc shook his head. "Fire? Sorry. I don't know what you're talking about."

"The wind shifted a couple of hours ago. The wildfire's moved out of Grace Canyon and is spreading this way. Looks like it might join up with the fire burning across the Kennedy ranch. The whole county could go up in flames."

Marc read fear beneath the patrol officer's professional calm, and irritation that he'd found a fool sleeping in a place that should be empty. There was also a strong sense of duty about getting the fool to safety.

"No, we didn't hear anyone knock earlier," Marc said.

Since he'd told the owner to forget about him two days ago, the man had left without delivering any warning.

"Thanks for waking us." Marc yawned and ran a hand across his freshly shaved head, like a man still not quite awake. "We'll get out of here right away."

"Get to the crossroads at Kennedyville, over Jessup Pass," the patrolman said. "Then head west."

West was the last place Marc intended to head. "Right. Thanks." He turned, and, for the man's benefit, said, "Honey, wake up. We have to get going."

While he spoke, he mentally sent suggestions for the man to remember that it was a married couple he'd rousted out of the motel if he remembered anything at all. He closed the door and rested his palms on it, willing the man to go away. After a minute Marc heard the rough cough of a car starting, then engine noise receding quickly in the distance.

Once he was sure he was alone, he stepped

outside and took a look around. He stopped in the center of the asphalt parking lot, with the low length of the motel building at his back. The lot was empty but for Josephine's Cherokee. The windows of the small diner and gas station across the street were dark, as were the few houses that made up the rest of the small town.

He looked up to where a crescent moon rode high in the sky and gave the old moon goddess a friendly nod. The crescent moon was part of Family heraldry, so he counted the sight as good luck.

He was going to need luck, he decided, when he looked at the sinister orange glow of fires on the horizon to the north and east. The desert night was cool, but he was aware of the heat from miles away.

He had no doubt why the fires were burning. He had to move quickly and put in as many miles as possible before daylight began to sap his strength. Though he could deal with daylight, life was easier at night.

He moved the Jeep across to the gas station and helped himself to a full tank. Then he packed their few belongings, and as much water as he could in the containers they'd used over the last couple of days. He consulted a map, aware of the minutes ticking away, but needing to be sure of routes.

After he'd made all the preparations, he picked up the still-sleeping Josephine and placed her gently in the passenger seat. Then he got in and drove, heading east, toward the ominous glow of the fire.

Chapter Eight

"This has got to stop," Jo muttered. The bed was bouncing, and there was a tang of smoke in the air. She wasn't really awake, but aware enough to be annoyed. "Cigarettes will kill you."

I'm not smoking.

Cage's voice in her head slowly rolled over her, like a velvet-covered boulder. It left her wanting more.

Say something else.

Prose or poetry?

She almost laughed. Almost laughing reminded her that she hadn't found much of anything humorous lately. That Cage could spark her sense of humor was—

Scary?

Let's not be that dramatic, she answered the thought.

Disturbing?

Oh, please! Merely disconcerting.

Don't let the bad guy make you laugh; he can use it against you?

Something like that.

And do what? Cause Death by Stand-Up? No one dies laughing, Josephine.

Keep talking, Cage. If I can't have chocolate, I'll take your voice.

Whoa. Where had that thought come from?

"You can have both," Cage said aloud.

He couldn't really read her thoughts, could he? He couldn't put himself in her head, her dreams?

She'd dreamed about the white room again, only this time Cage had been there with her. She hated that place. It was all very symbolic of being a prisoner, and the sterile setting she got trapped in during her dreams also reminded her of the hospital. Understanding what her subconscious had dragged up didn't make the place seem less real, though. This time the dream hadn't been about pain, but sex.

"Power games, either way."

Jo finally opened her eyes.

She realized that she was out of the motel room at last. The Jeep was bumping along a back road in the middle of the night. A high ridge reared up on the left, while flatter ground rolled off to the right. An ominous snake of light followed the line of the ridge. The smell of smoke came from that way.

Her mouth was dry from fear when she spoke. "That's one of the fires I read about."

"Yeah."

How could he sound so calm? "What the hell are you doing?" she demanded.

"Don't worry," he answered. "The hills are between it and us."

Oh, God, what was the wind like out there? Direction, speed? The brush and trees were dry, very, very dry. And the dry streambeds weren't wide enough to make good firebreaks this time of year.

"Fire can jump," she told him. "The wind can whip it into a storm. Stop the car, City Mouse, and let me drive. I'm getting us out of here."

Marc took umbrage at her thinking he didn't know what he was doing, even if he didn't, exactly. "We'll be okay."

"People do not run toward infernos, Cage." She spoke slowly and carefully, as though explaining to a child.

He was aware of how hard she was holding down the urge to panic and how annoyed she was at him for always keeping her on the edge of it.

"It can't be helped," he explained. "The fires

have been set to flush me out, and that's not going to happen. So we go opposite the way any sane person would go."

"Into the wildfire?" Her voice rose with the words.

"Around the fire. Stay calm; we can do this."

"*We*? I didn't volunteer to be broiled." Josephine took several deep breaths, but her agitation didn't lessen. "And what do you mean, the fires were set to flush you out?" Was he crazy?

She looked ahead and noticed that the headlights weren't on though she could see the road by the glow of the death trap over the ridge. "Why aren't the headlights on?"

"So we won't be seen from above by circling planes. If they have nightscopes, it might not help, but the heat from the wildfire might make the scopes useless."

Jo stared at Cage in disbelief. "This *isn't* about you."

"Yeah. It is."

"You cannot really believe that the fires were set because of you."

He looked at her with his head tilted to the side. "Impressive, isn't it? They really want me back."

"The police don't set fires to help them with manhunts."

"We're not escaping the police. And I'm not a man." He looked at the road again, then at the ridge. "I think the fire's coming over the hill up ahead."

While she sat pressed back against her seat, trying to take in the enormity of her captor's insanity, he switched the Jeep into four-wheel drive and eased the SUV off the road to drive cross-country. The going was rough, but the vehicle was tough, and Cage drove very carefully.

Jo could make out very little of what lay in their path. "I hope you can see in the dark," she muttered, as the Jeep bumped and swayed over landscape and low bushes.

"No problem."

Of course not. He isn't a man.

She couldn't stop the crazed giggle that rose in her throat. She put her hands over her mouth, breathed through her nose, and fought giving in to hysteria. She was going to have a good fit when the chance finally arose.

As Jo wondered exactly what Cage thought he was, she ran a thumb over her slightly aching right wrist. That brought back a vague memory.

Had he bitten her? She concentrated, trying to draw up memories that were oddly fuzzy. Had he been drugging her? She'd certainly been sleeping a lot. But she had a strong feeling that he'd bitten her, twice—and when he did, things went all erotic on her. Something left her shaken, out of control and—all right, admit it—fully satisfied. There was a deep sharing that took place. And the sharing of thoughts and dreams wasn't in her imagination.

Or was it? She hadn't been too stable before Cage happened to her. All she could be sure of was that, once again, she was out in the desert at the wrong place and time.

"There's more than one fire," she told the kidnapper driving her Jeep.

"I know."

"If they connect, we're going to be in more trouble than we already are."

Marc finally grew exasperated. Didn't she know he was doing the best he could? Maybe it was risky, but it was the only way he could elude his pursuers. "You're a city girl from Phoenix. How do you know so much about fires?"

"I've camped all over the Southwest all my life," she answered.

"Bet you were a Girl Scout. Got a badge in firefighting?"

"I certainly was a Scout," she responded proudly. "Besides, my family business is flying. I used to fly charter helicopters and transports for the BLM every summer."

"BLM?"

"Bureau of Land Management. I've taken fire-fighters and supplies in and out of fire areas since I was a teenager. I've seen fires from the air and from the ground, and I'd rather not see this one at all."

Her anger hit him like a hot wind off one of those blazes, and he knew that she had good reason to fear for her life. While fire could kill him, it would take far more than third degree burn damage and far longer exposure to flame than it would her before it would kill him. Josephine was fragile mortal skin and bone, and she knew exactly what fire could do to her.

He worried about her, but there was more at stake than saving their skins. He kept on driving, carefully avoiding cacti and boulders, and the many creatures out there that were afraid for their lives. Since Josephine was an empath, maybe part of her fear was a reaction to the mood of the desert animals. Even if it was hard on her in a dangerous situation, Marc admired his woman's gifts.

He also admired how she'd reacted when he questioned her competence. She was no cream puff. "You fly helicopters?" he asked, trying to distract them both from the fire behind them. "That's cool."

"Yeah," was her flat answer.

He could almost feel the temperature in the Jeep go down. She didn't want to talk about flying, but maybe she needed to. He persisted. "Been flying long? What kinds of craft are you rated for?"

"Planes, copters. It's a job. It was a job. I'm never getting in a plane again."

"It wasn't your fault your plane crashed."

"How do you know?"

"It's understandable that you're scared to get in the air again. But when you fall off a horse you get back on, right? It's the same with anything that scares you."

Anger, regret, fear, and pain seethed through her. "When you fall off a horse, you don't kill other people," she finally answered. "When you take responsibility for other people's lives, and fail—" Her voice trailed off into a painful sigh.

Why did she have to bring up taking responsibility for somebody else?

"You might want to think about yourself," he suggested. "Do you want to fly again?"

"This isn't exactly a good time for me to think about my future, now, is it?"

Her annoyance flicked against his senses, and her words stung.

Marc figured it was time to shut up and drive, something that was increasingly difficult, even with his excellent night vision. It wasn't just the rough terrain; the night was alive with animals fleeing for their lives. He was aware not only of their movement, but of racing hearts, and the scent of fear mixed with smoke.

When one scent grew stronger than the others, Marc rolled down his window and took a deep breath of the acrid air. There was something out there—

Josephine coughed. "Smells like a fox."

"Yeah," Marc answered, as a large animal dashed in front of the Jeep.

"What was that?"

"A fox."

Jo peered through the windshield. "Too big to be a fox. It doesn't look like a coyote, though. It's circling back. Maybe it wants to hitch a ride."

"Maybe."

A quick glance at Cage told her that her captor wasn't joking. He was frowning furiously, his gaze swinging from side to side. When the large animal dashed in front of the Jeep again, Cage swore under his breath. Then he rolled up the window and stepped on the gas.

His reaction sent a shiver up her spine. "What's out there?" she asked.

"Nothing." He stared straight ahead, his jaw set so hard that his neck muscles strained.

A howl sounded behind them, mournful, afraid.

"Did you hear that?"

"No."

"If you didn't hear it—"

"Blast!" Cage slammed hard on the brakes. When the Jeep jolted to a halt, he growled, "Wait here."

The door opened and slammed shut, and Cage was gone into the night. Jo stared after him, her mouth open in surprise. After a few seconds she looked around, all too aware of the danger in which he'd left her.

"Great. *Now* he gives me an opportunity to escape."

Chapter Nine

Cage sprinted back to the Jeep before Jo could make up her mind to climb into the driver's seat. She was almost grateful he didn't give her time to work through whether or not she should leave him to take his chances with the fire.

He wasn't alone, but was carrying a small woman in his arms. A slender red-haired man trotted along beside him. The fact that the couple were naked was almost as surprising as their being out here in the first place.

Cage opened the back door and set the woman down, then he got behind the wheel. The man climbed in after her and took the moaning woman in his arms. Cage put the Jeep in gear and made a wide turn, heading back toward the road. He looked straight ahead, grim and angry. Jo was consumed with equal parts relief and curiosity, but didn't dare ask any questions when frustration was boiling off Cage in a psychic shock wave.

She turned to look at the couple in the backseat, and saw that the woman was heavily pregnant.

"Thank you," the naked red-haired man said. "We were trapped. If you hadn't come along—"

"How did you get out here?" Jo blurted out. "Why are you here? Why are you naked?" Maybe that wasn't any of her business, but it was a natural question. "Are you in labor?" she asked the woman. The woman nodded, then turned her head, burying her face against the man's bare shoulder.

"Know anything about birthin' babies, Girl Scout?" Cage asked her.

"No," she answered. He was driving faster back than he had into the desert. Jo was grateful that he was heading for the road, and for the seat belt that secured her. All this jostling around couldn't be good for the woman. "Do you know anything about birthing babies, Cage?"

"Do I look like a midwife?"

"More like an angel," the man in back said. "You saved our lives, Prime." The man then said something in a language Jo didn't understand.

Cage answered. "Not my dialect. I'm not

Clan, furball." Jo saw a look of fear flash over the man's sharply triangular face. It changed to relief when Cage added, "I'm not Tribe, either."

"Yes, of course. I and my mate will find a way to repay your kindness."

"I know you will," Cage answered.

Jo felt like she could learn a lot from this conversation, if only she had the key to translate what they were actually talking about. The language was English, but she felt like she was eavesdropping on a pair from a foreign culture.

"You know each other?" she asked.

The Jeep reached the road, and Cage turned onto it, thankfully heading away from the fire. When he floored it, Jo sighed with relief. The woman let out another loud moan.

"We better get her to a hospital," Jo said.

"No need." The man gently massaged the woman's abdomen. "All we need is to be safely away from the firestorm. We left our car at a convenience store outside Kennedyville. Take us to our car, and we'll be fine."

"Okay," Cage agreed.

"She needs a doctor," Jo insisted, but was ignored.

"What the hell were you doing out here?" Cage asked.

"We wanted to have the baby the old-fashioned way. So we hiked out into the desert, made a den." He sighed, and rubbed his cheek against the woman's head. "It seemed like a good idea at the time."

Jo noticed that the pregnant woman also had red hair. And there was something odd about the couple, something fey and feral. She recalled the musky smell of fox, and the creature that had circled the Jeep before Cage stopped and jumped out of the SUV. There'd been a flash of movement ahead of him, hadn't there? Had he followed the fox? And what did the red-haired naked guy mean by making a den?

"Uh—"

"Don't ask," Cage cut her off before she could ask. "It's saner that way."

Instead of focusing on the utter weirdness of the couple, Jo took some comfort in the fact that Cage had saved them. Not only had he stopped for the pair, he was taking them to safety, even though he believed he was risking his own freedom. It was obvious he wasn't happy about this decision to act humanely, but he was doing it—so he couldn't be all bad, right? Which had to bode well for her own safety?

A warm glow spread through her, despite her fears and reservations, and she couldn't help but look at Cage with reluctant admiration. Which was stupid, considering they shouldn't have been out in the desert with the wildfire in the first place. But if they hadn't been, the pair in the backseat would likely have died. Maybe it was fate.

Fate? Oh, boy. Maybe the events of the last few days had driven her crazy, too. And why was she sitting here thinking too much, when she should be doing something to *save* herself? There were people in the backseat, for God's sake! She could find a way ask them to help her, to let them know she was a prisoner. They could warn the authorities—

Cage's big hand landed on Jo's thigh. Its weight and warmth startled her. He squeezed gently, and that was all the warning she needed. *Not a word,* that touch said, *not a sign, not a look or movement out of place.* Cage would only go so far in this act of kindness; he already believed he was risking his own freedom. She dared not push him, and put the pregnant woman's safety at risk.

He gave her a warning glance, and she gave a sharp nod in return. He smiled a little. Bastard. When she tried to push his hand away, he slipped it higher up her thigh.

"Keep your hands on the wheel and your eyes on the road," Jo said.

The woman gave out a long, loud moan.

"Faster, Prime," the man said. "Please."

"Prime what?" Jo asked.

"He is Prime," the man answered. "Don't you know your own mate's bloodline, woman?"

"You take care of your mate, and I'll take care of mine," Cage told him. "We're coming up on a crossroads," he added.

"It's not far beyond that."

They'd passed a scattering of dark and deserted buildings straddling the roadside a few minutes before, and Jo suddenly realized that it was the place where Cage had kept her prisoner. Where were they, anyway? She didn't recognize the name Kennedyville, though she'd probably flown over the place plenty of times.

There were maps in the glove compartment. If she could get a look at one, it would help her get her bearings. Knowing where she was and what day it was might help her regain a sense of reality.

Well, it was *her* Jeep. Was she supposed to ask permission? Or furtively sneak a look at one of her own possessions when Cage wasn't looking? Maybe she was a mess, but she wasn't a mouse, city or country. She'd been forced into a scary situation, but she'd been scared before and held it together, until she hit the ground. Then there'd been pain and suffering and guilt, which she'd been almost starting to work through when this jerk came along. What she had to do now was get it together, and get out.

Jo pushed Cage's hand away, then leaned forward and opened the glove compartment, taking out a map and small flashlight.

"What are you doing?"

"Navigating," she told him.

He said nothing, so she concentrated on the map while Cage drove over increasingly rough road that switchbacked along the side of a mountain. She really wished he'd turn the headlights on, even if he obviously wasn't having trouble seeing. The people in the back huddled together silently, except for occasional distressed sounds from the woman in labor. Jo winced in sympathy at every sound she made.

After a few minutes of studying the map by dim light in the bouncing vehicle, Jo announced, "Near as I can figure, we're heading into the Jessup Mountains." They hadn't traveled far from where she'd been captured and were heading back that way.

"I could have told you that," Cage said. They crested the mountain as he spoke and started down. Beyond the pass the road was straighter, if not much smoother, and he put on more speed.

Jo flicked off the flashlight and studied his hard-jawed profile. "But would you have?"

He gave a one-shoulder shrug. "Hard to say."

The man in back said, "There! Up there. On the left. Hurry!"

"I see it."

Jo peered through the windshield, but had no clue what the men saw. It was at least another half mile before she made out the dark outline of a large, flat-roofed building up ahead. She didn't see the car near the building until Cage pulled up beside it in the small parking lot.

"Stay here," he told her once again, and got out of the Jeep.

Marc reached for the handle, but the rear door opened before he could touch it. He stepped back and let the pair he knew were werefoxes out of the Jeep, then followed as the male rushed to get his mate settled in their own vehicle.

"Wait a minute," Marc called, as the male got behind the wheel.

The male put down the window and stuck his head out. "Hurry. I have to get her home."

"I know." Marc rubbed his jaw. He was loath to trust anyone outside his Family with information, but sometimes you had no choice. "Are you Affiliated?"

The fox nodded. "Reynard Clan, House Isabeau."

Okay. That wasn't so bad. The Reynards were known as the noblest of the clean-living, good-guy vampire clans. And it made sense that a werefox would be allied to the Reynards.

"How's your memory?" he asked.

"Perfect. If you want me to get a message to the Clan, tell me and let me go."

"Thanks." Marc spoke a few words in his own language, preferring to speak from vampire to vampire. Somebody in the Clan would be able to translate and pass the information on to his own people.

"Got that?" The werefox repeated the message back to him. "Good," Marc said, and stepped back from the car.

The werefox started the engine, just as the Jeep engine came to life a few yards behind him.

Marc spun around, and his deep-voiced shout filled the night. "Hey!"

Dust and pebbles flew up in the Jeep's wake as Josephine raced out of the parking lot.

Marc had the keys to the Jeep in his hand, and the second set in his pocket. She must have had a third set secreted in the SUV.

He lunged toward the werefox's car, but it was already moving, and he couldn't grab the door handle. Marc shook a fist as the foxes drove away. Seemed like no good deed went unpunished.

Left alone, he howled in frustration and pain at being stranded right back where he'd started nearly a week ago. Only now he was worse off than before.

"Josephine!" The word was a painful howl of betrayal, grief, and rage.

Then he took a deep breath, gathered all his energy, and began to run after the woman fleeing him into the fading night.

Chapter Ten

Jo didn't know why she was crying as she drove away. She'd started crying the moment Cage got out of the Jeep, because she knew what she had to do and almost didn't have the strength to leave him.

"Stupid!" She swiped a hand across her eyes. She could barely see as it was, and she was shaking so hard she could hardly grip the steering wheel. Her hands were sweaty, her heart was pounding as adrenaline and fear pumped through her.

There was a voice in her head screaming that if she left him, he'd die, and the voice wasn't his. And that was just crazy!

When his deep bellow of pain pierced the night behind her, she told herself it was her imagination. She had to get away. This was no time to think, no time to feel remorse. Even if she did, she'd get over it once she was out from under Cage's strange influence.

Oh, my God! What if he takes those people prisoner? The thought struck her like a blow to the stomach.

Was she trading their freedom for hers? Why hadn't she thought of that? She risked a quick look in the rearview mirror and sighed in relief when she saw that the other car was heading in the opposite direction. If Cage had forced his way into their vehicle he'd be chasing her, right? He'd try to stop her from reaching the authorities. Though she honestly didn't believe he'd harm the pregnant woman he'd rescued.

So, they were safe. She was safe.

But what was that shadow in the road ahead of her? A fallen boulder? Why was it so dark?

"Because you haven't turned the headlights on, fool."

It was like riding around in the dark had become normal for her because it was normal for Cage.

She flipped on the lights, squinting into the sudden brightness. The high beams illuminated a man standing in the center of the road ahead of her.

Jo screamed.

Cage's muscles glistened with sweat. His white

T-shirt clung to his heaving chest, and the eyes glaring directly at her were glowing fiery red.

Jo could only stare unbelievingly at the apparition before her. He held his hands up and shouted something. Then she realized that the Jeep was heading straight toward him and that he wasn't going to get out of the way. She jerked the wheel hard right, heading off the road and out of control.

Cage jumped onto the hood as the Jeep plunged down a short embankment and rode the SUV like a wild bull as it plowed forward. *Brake!* He shouted inside her head. *Put your hands on the wheel and your foot on the brake!*

Jo realized that her hands were covering her open mouth and hysteria was quenched by the ingrained emergency calm she'd learned as a pilot. Her hands found and fought the wheel, her foot found the brake. Within moments she brought the Jeep to a halt and turned off the engine.

It was only then that she wondered why she'd gone out of her way not to run over the man who'd pursued her.

A vision of what might have happened hit her hard, and she flew out of the Jeep and was on Cage even as he jumped off the hood to confront her.

"Idiot!" She grabbed him by the shoulders. He was too big for her to shake, but that didn't stop her from trying. "You idiot!"

"Me?" he shouted back. "You—"

"You could have been killed!"

The heat of the energy he'd burned racing ahead of the Jeep came off him in waves. He was panting, and she knew instinctively that he'd hurt himself with so much exertion. The hard muscles under her hands quivered with fatigue and fury.

"I could have killed you!"

Josephine's genuine distress pierced the anger that had driven him to nearly kill himself to get to her.

"Woman, what is the matter with you?" he demanded. He was seeing the world in pulsing red, everything but her. She was a bright, constant flame. His head was throbbing, his control hanging by a thread.

"The matter with me? I was trying to escape!"

"I know. What are you so upset about?"

"You could have been hurt."

"Yeah—but—I'm the bad guy!"

He couldn't help but be furious at her running. He couldn't help but give chase. What he found hard to understand was that she was upset *because* he might have been hurt by her. It messed up his mind, made everything complicated. How could he feel betrayed when she was so worried about his safety?

"You drive me crazy," he told her.

"Me? This is all your fault!"

"I know." He pulled her close. Then closer still. He wanted her. He wanted her so badly, it hurt. "I'm sorry."

He'd been sane once, hadn't he? Before he met her. Before they took him away and tortured all the civilization out of him. He'd been brought down to basic needs, and wanting Josephine was as basic a need as he was ever going to experience.

His head was pounding from exertion as much as confusion. As the adrenaline rush of anger wore off, the thirst roared to life. The need for blood mixed with the thirst for sex, and lust, won out. All his senses focused into acute awareness of the woman he held. She was soft, fragile, so very alive. The strength of her emotions was intoxicating even as they pounded at him with a mix of anger, fear, and overwhelming concern.

In a confused, mad way she cared for him, and that added more fuel to his desire. "Josephine."

Jo lifted her head off his chest at Cage's rough whisper, both body and mind responding to the need in his voice. When he bent to kiss her she opened her mouth, and something wild tore loose inside her when their lips touched. He was male, hard, huge, dominant, and demanding. All the danger and power he exuded was intoxicating. Kissing him, she tasted dark, heady wine. She responded, female to male, and she *wanted*— every touch, every taste, every rough caress, every hard kiss. Her hands moved over his smooth, hard, hot muscles, as fiercely intent on sensation as he was.

They sank to their knees onto the hard earth. His hands roamed up under her shirt to stroke her breasts, across her back, then to push down her shorts and cup her bare bottom. Every touch took her deeper into her own need. She ground her hips against his, and he moaned and rose to his feet, bringing her up with him. Her head spun, and she clutched desperately to his straining arms as he picked her up and moved to the Jeep.

"What?" she asked, pulling away when he would have kissed her again. Fear shot through her.

He calmed it with a whisper. "Scorpions. Snakes." He settled her in the backseat and climbed in on top of her.

Night creatures, she thought, of course. Like him. Dangerous and deadly, but not if you treated them right.

"Cage." She spoke his name on a moan, a sound of anguished longing and desperate pleading.

"Josephine."

His need poured into her, hers boiled up from deep inside her. The blending sparked fire, and hunger.

She reached for him, and her fingers scraped across the rough stubble of his shaved head. Sparks shot through her, sizzled through her nerve endings. The salty tang of fresh sweat on his skin excited her. Basic, primal need battered her. He moved, half-sitting to pull off his shirt and unfasten his trousers.

When he leaned close again she ran her hands over his hard chest and belly, reveling in the feel of his naked skin. "Beautiful." His big, solid body filled the cramped back of the SUV, filled the darkness with overwhelming sensory impressions.

His mouth came down on hers, then he nuzzled her breasts, suckled her nipples. Her back arched, and the breath caught in her throat as desire built deep inside her.

He grasped her by the hips, fitting her beneath him. *"Josephine."*

Then with one hard push he was inside her, filling her. When his hips began to pump, she went wild. She arched up, meeting every swift, powerful stroke, her fingers pressing deep into his shoulders. All she could do was ride the building pleasure. He was a hurricane, and she needed the storm washing over her. She needed him.

She might have screamed when the first orgasm took her. Someone did, but she was too taken with pleasure to be sure who made the sound, or even who was Cage and who was Jo. All she knew when the wave of ecstasy passed was that her desire wasn't sated yet.

"More. Give me *more*."

The answer was a deep, animal growl, a prick of pain on her breast. A wave of pleasure immediately washed through her, took her up over the edge again. There was no coming down this time. Another peak came immediately, then higher to another, and another.

Chapter Eleven

Jo opened her eyes, blinked, and discovered Cage's shaved head resting on her shoulder. Her naked shoulder. "Oh, boy."

She almost wished she hadn't woken up, and not just because of the confusion that came with conscious thought. She had a crick in her neck, and her back ached, and that was only the beginning of the places that felt used and abused. She was beginning to understand the old-fashioned term of "being taken," and thought that if she soaked in a very hot tub of water for a couple of days, the muscle aches might begin to go away.

She didn't feel violated; she was just sore. It was a long time since she'd had sex, and she'd never had it in such close quarters. Cage's size made it even more cramped. He weighed her down now, flattened her, and in so many more ways than physical.

He still slept, sated, satisfied. Full. He'd taken her—in more ways than physical.

Taken, yes.

She sighed, a deep, weary exhalation. She found that she was cradling his head on her shoulder, her fingers slowly stroking the back of his shaved head. She didn't know why she liked the way it felt. She'd never been with a man with a shaved head before; it was rather exotic, in a peach-fuzzy sort of way.

I have no reason to like this man, she reminded herself. *What's to like, other than the fact that he hasn't killed me yet?*

And he hasn't raped me.

She couldn't blame him for what they'd done. She didn't blame herself, either. Later she might be embarrassed, even appalled, but it was only an adrenaline-driven chemical reaction on both their parts. She didn't want to think about it. She certainly didn't want to dredge up details from her memory.

Right now she just wanted to get comfortable, to stretch out and go to sleep. It was just after dawn, and the coolness of the desert night was already slipping away. She wondered if *she* could slip away, if she had the strength to. It wasn't that she lacked the will, it was that she felt weak, drained.

The man somehow took the energy out of her. It made her so tired. Tired and hungry. She wanted to eat a steak and sleep for a good long time. The man somehow made her crave meat. If there was anything she should blame him for, it was her abandonment of over a decade of being a vegetarian.

"I'm hungry," she said aloud, and was surprised at how rough her voice was. Maybe she *had* been the one screaming with pleasure—but she didn't want to think about that.

Marc woke up feeling Josephine's hunger; he was also aware of the growing daylight on his skin. Time to get dressed and get going. But the urge to care for her needs first was almost overwhelming. The woman beneath him was gentle and vulnerable and his to protect. It was her gentleness that led to what had happened between them.

All right, that wasn't precisely true. He'd intended to have her when he hunted her down; it was his right.

But then she'd turned it all around with her concern for his safety, her fear of hurting him. That turned his anger-born passion into something far more dangerous—for him, if not for her. By the time he carried her to the backseat of the Jeep, he'd had to have her because he couldn't live another minute without making love to her. But he hadn't been gentle or kind about it.

He lifted his head and looked at her, and they looked at each other warily for long seconds. He wanted to kiss her. But he didn't know what to expect.

"Am I supposed to apologize?" he asked.

She considered this very seriously before she said, "Let's call it an act of temporary insanity."

"I can go with that." It was easier to keep emotions out of this.

He didn't know why he should apologize for sex, anyway. It was a Prime's right to take pleasure, and a Prime's duty to give pleasure. He knew how well he'd performed on both counts.

It was just that . . . he hadn't been very nice about it.

He rubbed his forehead against Josephine's shoulder. "Goddess, I'm turning into a wimp."

"You could get off me," she suggested. "You can't be any more comfortable than I am."

He certainly wasn't—not with the way he was positioned between her open legs, and growing hard, being so close, so aware . . .

He took a deep breath and pried himself off her and forced his body to calm down. Never mind what he wanted to do; they had to get out of here. He put his head in his hands and rubbed his temples. The growing light was giving him a hell of a headache. And here he was, back near where he'd found her. He didn't know how long or how far he'd run before that night, but he was worried that it hadn't been far enough. Though he'd tried to get away from danger, it felt like he was running back toward a trap. Stupid hippie werefoxes. He shouldn't have stopped for them.

"What's wrong, Cage?"

He turned his head to look at her. She'd sat up as well, and had found the T-shirt and bra he'd dropped on the floor. Her blond hair was tousled, and there were dark circles under her eyes, but she didn't look too much the worse for wear.

"It all seems futile this morning," he answered her. "Life. Everything."

"You should have a cup of coffee," she advised. "It generally helps my mood in the morning." She stretched.

"I'll consider it." He put his hand around her outstretched wrist and turned her toward him. "Just how many sets of car keys do you have?"

She smiled. "I don't think I'm going to answer that."

"Fine." He shook a large index finger under her nose. "Don't try that trick on me again. Stay here," he ordered, and got out of the Jeep.

"You're always saying that," she said, and followed him out. "You're not the only one who has to pee, you know," she added, as they went to opposite sides of the Jeep.

She didn't try to run again while he got dressed. When he got into the front and found the sunglasses he desperately needed, she climbed into the backseat, and told him, "I'm going to take a nap. Wake me up when you've found food."

"Your wish is my command."

"Liar."

Actually, it was. He just didn't dare let her know it.

She woke up inside the stripped-down fuselage of an airplane. She recognized the old metal bones arching overhead the instant she opened her eyes. As she lurched upright, her mouth opened in a scream of panic. But Cage's hand covered her mouth before any sound came out.

She was in a plane!

She couldn't be in a plane! Never again!

She fought to get out, but he held her down. Kept her inside. Spots danced in front of her eyes, and darkness wavered on the periphery of her vision, but she couldn't stop trying to scream.

Let me out! Let me out! Let me out!

Calm down, it's all right. What is the matter with you?

Get me off. I can't—I can't—

Can't what?

An airplane. I can't be on an airplane. We'll fall. We'll crash. I can't—

You can't crash. We're not flying. It's just an old wreck in an abandoned boneyard. You're a pilot—you know about boneyards.

Of course she did. They dotted the desert landscape, if you knew where to look for them. She began to calm down. He eased his hand away, and she gasped in air, then found herself panting from the lack of it.

His hand hovered near her mouth. "Don't scream," Cage said. "Just take slow, even breaths—and don't scream."

"Why not?" she asked when she could speak. "If the place is abandoned?"

"It hurts my delicate ears." He sat back on his heels. "Feeling better?" She nodded. "I should have realized you might have a strong reaction to being in an airplane. Sorry." He gestured around the bare interior of the hulk. "Maybe you should consider this therapy."

She took a good look around as well. "I consider it a B-29."

He rose to his feet and turned around slowly. "Really? This is a World War II bomber? How do you know?"

She was amazed by his sudden enthusiasm. "Because I know airplanes."

He sat down cross-legged in front of her. "And I'm into history. Tell me about this plane."

She shrugged. "It's a bomber. From World War II. Tell me what we're doing here."

"Camping out. I brought in all your gear from the Jeep; we stopped for groceries while you slept. Want a ham sandwich?"

She finally noticed that she was sitting on her sleeping bag. Her stomach growled when he mentioned food. "Yes. And water." She rubbed her throat. With the heat, she was dying of thirst.

The metal body of the plane provided shade, but it magnified the heat. Glancing toward the gaping hole where the cockpit window used to be, she judged by the light that it was late afternoon. At least she could see clear blue sky and the hazy outline of mountains in the distance; this didn't have the claustrophobic quality of the motel room. She didn't even mind that she was in an airplane, now that she was fully awake.

While he moved to her cooler, she sighed in frustration. Why was she always asleep when they were around other people? Did he give her some kind of drug to keep her knocked out whenever he needed? Was it magic?

"Hypnotism," he said, turning back with his hands full. He looked at her over the rim of the sunglasses he always wore in the daytime. "Or something like it."

She took the sandwich and wolfed it down, then gulped the cold water from the liter bottle he gave her. He had another sandwich waiting when she finished drinking. She polished the second one off quickly as well.

"Cookies?" he asked, when she was finished. He held up a bag of Oreos.

She eagerly reached out both hands for them.

He gave a rumbling chuckle, then sat down by her and opened the cookie bag. "You have to share." He took one and popped it in his mouth before handing the bag to her.

"You're eating that wrong," she told him, and twisted the chocolate cookies apart so she could lick the white filling off first. "Oreos aren't just food, they're a culinary experience."

"Oysters are a culinary experience," he said. "That's a cookie."

"Oysters." She made a face. "Oh, God."

"Goddess," he said. "My people worship a goddess."

She recalled that he'd mentioned a goddess before, though she couldn't remember when or where. "You're a Wiccan?"

He looked puzzled by the word for a moment, then said, "No. My people avoid witches as much as we do everyone else, unless we marry them. We Primes like our women psychic."

There was that word again—Prime. And talk of his *people,* and psychic powers. "Who are you, Cage? Who are your people?"

He stared silently into the shadows for a minute, then took off the sunglasses and looked at her intently. His eyes were as dark as triple espresso.

"I'm a Prime of Family Caeg. C-a-e-g. It means door. Our kind are very into heraldry, tradition, respecting our past, and preserving our ways. The Family's symbol is a crescent moon behind a tree branch—very shadowy and mysterious. The Caeg Family crest is a heavy old iron-bound castle door. It's important to me, being a member of my Family within the Families. That's who I am." He tilted his head and gave a faint shrug. "And not a word of that makes any sense to you."

"It made a sort of sense, if you're into genealogy and coats of arms and stuff like that. Which apparently you are."

"I know where I come from. That's important. Family is important. Especially for a small ethnic minority trying to get by among strangers."

"Now, doesn't that sound dramatic."

Another of his shrugs. "That's us. Tight-knit, insular, urban, living in the shadows and out of sight, on the fringes."

"What about your great-grandmother's farm? That doesn't sound urban or insular."

"She is an exception," he answered. "And her place is a refuge, a safe place for kids to come of age. It takes a while for our children to mature," he added.

Jo gathered from Cage's solemn attitude that he had just revealed a profound and closely guarded secret to her, but she had no clue as to why it was so important. She still didn't know anything about Cage, the man. For a moment she couldn't even recall his first name, though she knew he'd told her what it was. "Marc," she said when it finally swam into her consciousness. "Your name is Marcus."

"A good Roman name."

"Are you Italian?"

"My family lived in Italy for many generations," he replied. "The family came to America in the 1800s and settled in New York. Before I was born."

"My family left New York long before I was born."

He smiled. "We have New York in common."

"And butter-and-egg men." It was perturbing

that she enjoyed finding that they had things in common, though he looked puzzled at what she'd said. "You asked if I knew what a butter-and-egg man was a few days ago. We were eating fried chicken at the time."

"Oh, right! How do we have that in common?"

"I gathered in context that your great-grandmother sold her farm produce to New York buyers. My great-grandfather was one of those buyers. That's part of my family history, passed down lo these many generations."

"Maybe they knew each other."

"Doubtful. He died in a nursing home out here in 1984. He was nearly ninety."

"Well, Gram's nearly three hundred, so it's possible."

Okay, so much for thinking they had anything in common. "You're crazy, Cage."

It was also disturbing that she was relaxed enough around her captor to comment on his sanity to his face. Having sex with someone did not automatically mean that you started trusting and liking him, she reminded herself firmly.

But she was still curious. She looked around the remains of the old plane. Through a hole in one side she made out a row of other scavenged and discarded aircraft. "How do you know about boneyards?" she asked him.

"I saw a show on them on the History Channel," he answered.

"Oh, lord," she moaned. "I'm being held prisoner by a geek."

"A tired one." He moved to the sleeping bag. "Scoot over," he said, and lay down.

He snagged her around the waist and pulled her to lie beside him, her back against his front, his arm held over her. The position was intimate, and comfortable. Even comforting—though that couldn't be right.

"You're getting sleepy," he said. "Very sleepy . . ."

"Cut that out."

He chuckled and kissed the back of her neck. It sent a pleasant shiver through her and a small ache of desire. *Oh, dear.*

Well, she *was* still tired, and had nothing better to do. So she closed her eyes, relaxed against the big man, and felt far too safe and contented as she drifted off to sleep.

Chapter Twelve

When she woke up hours later, Jo found that she was lying face-to-face with Cage, her head on his shoulder. His arm was still around her, and hers was now around him. For a moment it felt exquisitely pleasant, then shock at being so comfortably intimate with him brought her completely awake.

It was only when she was fully alert that she realized that it was night, and the temperature had dropped like a rock. They'd cuddled together in their sleep like a pair of animals to share body heat.

That was a *much* better explanation than thinking they'd cuddled together for mutual comfort— and because the way their bodies fit together felt nice.

She sensed that he was awake; but he did nothing to stop her when she slowly rolled away and sat up even more slowly. She moved like an old woman, stiff and aching from the cold and from the hard floor. One foot was asleep, and when she rose carefully to her feet, her hips and thighs were sore.

Cage sat up as she stood, stretched, and groaned. "You okay?"

"I may never walk again. And don't give me that smug look, Cage, this isn't all your doing."

"It's too dark for you to tell I'm looking smug."

"I can feel smugness waves from your direction."

"That is only because you are a natural-born empath."

She didn't feel particularly empathic lately, not since he had shown up. In a way, this lack of picking up other people's emotional leakage was a blessing. Then again, thanks to Cage she'd pretty much been isolated from people, so there was no one but him for her to focus on.

"And, I," he went on, "am a natural-born—"

"Killer?"

"Stud."

"Don't give yourself too much credit for my condition," she told him, rolling her stiff shoulders, then stretching her arms over her head. "I'm full of pins and plastic, and nothing works right anymore."

"It'll get better," he assured her. "That I can promise you."

The sincerity in his deep voice touched her, reassured her as no promise from any doctor had managed to do, and she didn't know why. And the doctors hadn't promised that she'd ever be completely free of pain. "Does this goddess of yours promise miracles?"

His dark voice was full of mesmerizing promise. "She gave me one when she led me to you."

For a moment Jo was caught up in his spell. "Are you *my* miracle?"

"Yes."

The conviction in his voice shook her, sending a hot rush of pleasure through her. Then she blinked and made herself break the spell. She turned her back on Cage and did some more stretches to work the kinks out.

When he came up silently behind her and put his hands on her shoulders, she went perfectly still. Warmth spread through her, though her nerves began to wind tighter and tighter. He was like a wall behind her, huge, unmovable, and completely commanding her attention. The hands on her shoulders were a warm, heavy weight. The touch was gentle, but she was conscious of the latent power that could snap her neck or squeeze the life out of her.

She realized that she was holding her breath and let it out sharply as his hands began to move. His thumbs rubbed circles against her shoulder blades while his fingers massaged her shoulders and neck. She went almost instantly from growing fear to nearly purring with pleasure.

"Better?" he asked after a few minutes.

She'd forgotten all about her sore muscles, and she was warm all over. "I think my bones are turning to jelly." He stopped and stepped away, and she rounded on him. "Hey!"

He chuckled at her complaint. "If your bones turn to jelly, I'll have to carry you everywhere."

She laughed. "Lazy."

"That's better," he said. He reached out and brushed the hair out of her face, then ran a thumb along her cheek. "You feel better when you laugh, when you're not concentrating on staying scared of me."

She found herself rubbing her face against his open palm and pulled back. "Well—you're a scary guy."

"Nobody can be scary all the time. It wastes energy, and I'm a lazy guy. You said so yourself."

What Marc felt right now was tempted, more than anything else. Tempted to make love to her, tempted to taste her again, and tempted to initiate her into the beginning of a true bond. She needed the healing and completion he could give her when she took his blood, and he wanted to offer it with all his heart—stupid and dangerous though that was. He owed her, and he cared for her.

But he *wasn't* stupid, and he was still very much in danger. They were still out there. He didn't just have to escape, he also had to make sure they were stopped so they couldn't harm his Family and his people. And he couldn't bring Josephine into his world until it was safe.

Besides, some of the drugs they'd given him might still be in his system. He wasn't going to risk tainting her with the chemicals that had nearly killed him. The pain and disorientation he had fought for so long were mostly gone, but he was still exhausted from thwarting Josephine's latest escape attempt. His physical condition had upgraded from near death to just being tired and sore. He was also horny, of course, but that was a Prime's natural condition.

"We have to go." He needed to get to a place where he could feel secure in using a telephone.

"Go? You want to abandon such luxury accommodations?"

"When I find you someplace with a bed and a bathroom, you'll thank me." He hefted the cooler and carried it out the large hole in the rear of the ancient airplane. When he came back, she'd rolled up the sleeping bag and was holding it and her duffel. He took them from her, and she followed him out to the Jeep.

To his surprise, she circled the dusty vehicle like she was giving it a thorough inspection. The moon overhead was bright enough for her to see fairly clearly.

When she circled back to the rear of the Jeep she said, "At least I didn't bang anything up when I drove off the road. However"—she gestured toward the license plate—"where did that come from?"

Her power of observation pleased him. "Stole it off a car from Nevada last time I stopped for gas."

"Why?"

He owed her the truth, even if she wasn't going to like it. "I don't want a cop to try to pull us over. You've been gone for over a week. I figured someone would have reported you missing by now, and there must be an APB out on your Jeep."

She went still for a moment, then turned a look of cold anger on him. "Of course my family's looking for me."

"You told me that your mom's a cop. There'll be extra energy put into the hunt for you."

"How clever of you to think of that. You have a fine criminal mind, Cage."

"Thank you. I learned most of my little tricks while working for the government." The desert night was cold, but they stood in tense silence for a moment. Finally, he asked, "You want to drive?"

"Of course I want to drive. It's my car."

"Okay."

After another long wait, she said, "Well?"

"Waiting to see if you have any more sets of car keys."

"No." She held out her hand.

He dropped keys into her palm, then they settled into the front seat. She started the engine and flipped on the headlights.

"I wish you wouldn't do that."

"I can't see in the dark."

"We're on a salt flat, with the moon shining on it. That's not dark." He reached over and turned the lights off. "You can do it, Josephine."

She didn't argue and put the engine in gear. "Which way?"

He pointed. "There's a break in the perimeter fence over there; it leads back to the road. Turn right at the road."

Jo drove silently for a while, enjoying being in control of the machine. Driving wasn't as satisfying as flying, but it had proved an adequate substitute since recovering from the crash.

Cage relaxed beside her, his head tilted back. He appeared to be napping.

After a while, though, he said, "You're beginning to miss flying."

"No," she answered through a throat tight with sudden pain.

"You're not the only empath in this car. I can feel you feeling wistful, Josephine."

"I miss my freedom," she answered. "That's all."

"If you say so."

He reached over and took her right hand, and twined his fingers with hers.

His touch brought her comfort, and it occurred to her that maybe her touch brought him comfort, as well. What the hell was he running from, anyway? She'd never asked him that, had she?

"Cage? Marcus?" she ventured.

"Hmmm?"

When he turned his head toward her, she thought she saw a faint glitter in his dark, dark eyes. She decided it was an effect of the moonlight bouncing off the dried salt crystals on the ground and turned her attention forward again.

"What are we doing out here?" she asked him. "Who are you running from? And why?"

Marc was acutely aware of the connection between them, even if she wasn't. He owed her his life and his sanity, and she deserved more than his simply having fixed the hole in her psychic shielding. The first night he'd found her, she'd been nearly as messed up as he'd been. When his mind had touched hers, he'd automatically found what he could use, but he had paid for what he took. He hadn't given her a choice, yet he had given her something she needed in return.

Sometimes, though, it was necessary to pay with the truth. Maybe he wanted to tell her, anyway.

"What are we doing out here? Trying to get away from the people I escaped from. Who am I running from? A group of renegade scientists trying to discover the secret of immortality. And why? Because I don't want to be a guinea pig. I don't want them to learn the secrets of immortality, because that would destroy my people, and probably yours, too."

Josephine angrily wrenched her hand away. "Dammit, Cage, why couldn't you just tell me you're a hit man on the run from the mob?"

"Because I'm not part of the mob."

"You said you were from a—a family."

"Not *that* kind of family." He was outraged that she would jump to such a conclusion, just because he was from the East Coast and had an Italian background. He was a vampire, not a mobster! "I thought you wanted the truth."

"Truth?" Her voice rose on the word. "Mad scientists?"

"I didn't say they were mad. Cold bastards, yes, but not crazy."

"Secret of eternal life?"

"There isn't any such thing, but they think so."

"Right. Immortality . . ."

Jo started laughing, and after a few seconds, she realized that she wasn't going to stop. She laughed so hard she started to cry. She barely managed to get the Jeep stopped before she totally collapsed.

Marc watched her reaction with annoyance and growing concern. Maybe he shouldn't have been so flippant, but the horror still haunted him and he'd found it hard to speak about it.

Still, her laughter stung.

"That does it. I'm driving."

Chapter Thirteen

Jo suddenly remembered the white room in the dream, and a painful gasp brought her laughter to a such a sudden halt that she choked for a moment.

She remembered horrible experiments—being strapped down, and needles and machines and cold, impersonal voices. Mad scientist nightmares.

But that was all they'd been—just bad dreams, symbols of her own captivity. After all the time she'd spent in the hospital, with the surgeries and rehab, of course her subconscious would create images that she found scary.

But what did her dreams have to do with Cage's claims of mad scientists and the search for immortality? Claims that sounded like some sort of comic book or Lara Croft scenario.

"Because they're my dreams, too," he said.

She turned in the car seat to glare at him. "Stop that!"

"What?" He grinned, and for a moment his eyes flashed red. Just for a moment. "Don't do that, Josephine."

"Do what?"

"Look away and pretend you didn't see it." He reached across the seat, took her chin, and made her face him. "You've noticed that I'm not like normal humans, but you've refused to think about it. I think it's time you thought about it."

"You can read my mind," she said. Then added, "Or at least I imagine that you can."

He arched an eyebrow. "Be honest, Josephine. Or I really will not let you drive anymore."

She stuck her tongue out at him, aware of how absurd the childish gesture was, but she couldn't help it. She was relaxing around him, and that was even more dangerous than letting herself fall into his fantasy world of super powers and . . . and . . . letting him get away with calling her Josephine.

It was such an ugly name, even though it had been in the family for generations. But Cage seemed to like it, and it sounded dignified and right in its old-fashioned way when spoken in his deep voice. Hell, Rapunzel or Snickerdoodle would sound good spoken in that voice. Yet she couldn't help but feel unique and special when he called her Josephine, like it was some secret love word between them.

Jo shook her head, realizing that she'd gone off on an inane tangent. She also knew that her mind had deliberately wandered, rather than do what Cage demanded, which was to examine how strange he really was. His speed was—his vision was—his psychic gifts were—

"Inhuman."

She was shocked that she'd said it, but he only shook his head.

"Not human," he said. "Not the same as inhuman. Or maybe it's easier for you to think of us as enhanced humans." He smiled wickedly. "Close enough to breed."

She ignored this remark. "Us? Your people? This family you've told me about."

"I haven't told you about my people because I can't share details yet. Just believe that the world isn't what it seems. You can accept that I'm different because you also have mental gifts that most people don't have."

Jo considered this very seriously. She couldn't logically explain her ability to read emotions, but until the ability turned on her recently it had been one she'd accepted, even enjoyed.

"Okay. I'll concede that the world is not

exactly as—normal—as most people would like
it to be. But what's the secret of immortality have
to do with—"

"I'm a lot older than I look," he said. "They
found out about me. A friend betrayed me and
he helped them trap me."

"Who are *they?* How old is older than you
look?"

He ignored her first question. "When I was a
Marine, it was in Vietnam. I'm somewhere
around eighty in human years, Josephine. That's
why they were experimenting on me."

"In some ways this all makes sense," she said
tentatively.

"But you don't completely believe me." He
sounded disappointed.

His disappointment bothered her. She was
beginning to trust him, wasn't she? He hadn't
hurt her; he'd helped those people. The man had
his good points. Except for the crazy parts.

"What about the police?" she asked. "What's
your reason for not going to the police?"

"If I can find a Clan Prime who's a cop, I'll tell
him. But I can't trust human cops."

"Why not?"

"Someone's spent a lot of money to finance the
research and keep it secret. A lot of money pays
for a lot of corruption. Cops can be bribed."

As daughter and sister to a pair of clean cops, she was offended that he assumed the police were easily corrupted. She also conceded that he *might* have a point.

"I need to think about it, okay?"

"I've got time."

Silence settled between them as she drove on. When they reached the road, she turned right as he'd instructed. He settled his head against the seat and closed his eyes. This road was sparsely traveled, but not deserted. The lights of the vehicles they passed were a reminder that she and Cage weren't the only people in the world.

"Don't you miss being around people?" she asked him after many miles of silence.

He cracked his eyes open. "I enjoy your company."

"Why? All I do is complain."

"But you do it so well. You also have trust issues."

She couldn't help but snort with laughter. Damn the man for making her situation seem funny.

"And you have problems with self-confidence, but that's understandable so soon after such a serious accident. I think we've made some progress there, but we'll keep working on them."

"Thank you for listing my shortcomings," she said sweetly.

"You're welcome. You're about to ask if I'm your captor or your shrink, and the answer is yes."

"And how am I supposed to report that on the insurance forms?"

"Not my problem." He pulled a map out of the glove compartment and didn't bother with the overhead light or the flashlight to read it. "Not too long to daylight. Pull over," he said after he finished with the map. "I'll drive now."

"I'm not tired."

"We're coming up on some towns," he told her. "So you understand why I'd feel better driving. Besides, it's time for you to get some sleep."

Jo stopped the Jeep on the shoulder of the narrow highway and turned a furious look on Cage. "You're going to knock me out now, aren't you?"

"Yeah."

"You blatant bastard!"

"Such language."

He leaned closer and took her face between his hands. His mouth brushed hers briefly, his lips very soft and tender. A spark of pleasure zinged through her, but it didn't quell her anger. She was tired of being manipulated. "I'm not letting you do this, Cage."

"It's safer for both of us."

"Safer for *you*."

"Josephine," he said, making her look into his deep, dark brown eyes. "Go to sleep."

"No!"

But he kept looking at her, and his voice whispered in her head, and she *was* tired, even without his telling her to be. Eventually, she did exactly what he told her to.

"This is bad." His deep voice echoed down the long, empty hallway.

"This is very bad," she agreed. She looked around fearfully. It might be empty, but the sense of watching menace was chilling. The air was freezing, and they were naked.

There was white everywhere—floor, walls, ceiling. The white hall stretched forever, lined with heavy white doors. Bare, bright lights glared down from overhead.

"My head hurts," she said.

"I can barely see," he admitted. "Light hurts."

She rubbed her bare arms. "The cold makes my skin burn."

He pulled her close, and they wrapped their arms around each other, sharing comfort and as much warmth as possible. His hard muscles were rigid with tension; she'd never felt so vulnerable. She couldn't feel safe being held like this, but she did feel loved. His concern helped.

He kissed her temple, then whispered in her ear, "We have to get out of here. We have to try."

She was afraid to try. She rested her forehead against his shoulder. It felt so hopeless. It felt like a trap. But she lifted her head and nodded. She'd try—for him.

"What do we do?" she asked.

"Try the doors."

He took her by the hand, and they walked down the long, long hall, bare feet slapping on the glacial white tiles. As they passed each white door, they tried to open it. Locked, one after another; they were all locked. The futility of it was wearing. Her fear grew with each step.

"Why won't they let us go?"

"We're valuable property. They need our blood."

At the sound of the word, the world changed. The harsh white light took on the glow of molten lava. All the white around them was suddenly splattered with scarlet. Blood ran down the walls and formed freezing rivulets on the floor. Their feet slipped in it as they continued walking, and they left a trail of bloody footprints behind them.

"They can follow us," she said.

"They already are," he answered.

They stopped, and as he listened carefully for the sounds of pursuers, all she could hear was the rapid sound of her own heartbeat. She wrapped her arms around him and rested her head on his chest. His heartbeat sounded slow, steady, and hers gradually stopped racing, matching the strong rhythm of his.

Soon, over the twin beating of their hearts, even she could hear the guards coming for them.

She held him tighter, never wanting to let him go. "I'm sorry. I should have believed you sooner."

He stroked his fingers through her short hair. "It's all right. I love you."

"I love you."

He pushed her gently away, took her hand again. "When I tell you to run, run. Don't look back."

"All right."

The sound of many heavy footsteps filled the cold air. The floor vibrated. Screams and shouts sounded all around them. The lights and the walls began to pulse. The white doors began to fade, slowly replaced by thick iron bars. Behind the bars, other prisoners howled in pain and terror. Skeletal arms reached out toward them.

She looked around at all the horror, all the people. "We have to help them."

He squeezed her hand tightly. "Run!"

They ran, barely keeping their footing on the blood-slick floor. She didn't look back, but she knew the guards were there, gaining on them with every step. They weren't going to escape.

"There!" he shouted.

A black door appeared ahead of them. They were close to the end of the corridor at last. A pair of guards reached him, grabbed him. He shook them off. As more came at him, he pushed her forward. He got them to the door and wrenched it open. There was nothing but void and blackness outside—and a long, long fall.

"No!" she screamed. "NO!" She couldn't go out there!

"You'll be safe. You have to be safe." The guards were all over him, beating him, chaining him. He ignored them. "I love you," he told her, and pushed her out into empty space. He slammed the door before the guards could reach her.

She screamed, and fell, and was alone—

And Jo woke up screaming in a bed, in a room, with Marcus writhing and moaning beside her.

Chapter Fourteen

It was the white room. No, the walls were white, but this wasn't—

Jo's heart was racing so hard, she thought it was about to hammer out of her chest. She could barely catch her breath for the panting gasps. She was covered in cold sweat, and the fear was so strong that she couldn't think about anything but the dream for long, horrible moments.

Knowing it was a dream didn't help. The reality of the horrible, cold white place was consuming. Even when the waking world began to come into focus, it was overlaid with a ghost vision of the long hall and the echo of footsteps chasing her.

She rubbed her shaking hands over her face, wiping away salty tears. She blinked the stinging moisture away and forced herself to be in this moment, this place, to be awake.

Gradually the room took on more reality than the dream. She didn't recognize anything around her, but it wasn't surprising to wake up in strange place with Cage. This one was slightly nicer than the last motel they'd stayed in. The bed didn't sag, and the walls were a freshly painted off-white. She was relieved that the color wasn't antiseptic, cold white.

Cage had left the bedside table lamp on, and its warm glow was reassuring. She swung her legs over the edge of the bed, and her feet touched soft carpet.

"Definitely better accommodations," she murmured.

Cage thrashed in his sleep, his arm waving wildly. It struck her, and Jo landed on her hands and knees on the carpet, stunned by the force of the blow. Above her Cage moaned, and the bedsprings creaked as he twisted and turned, fighting some invisible enemy.

Not invisible to him, she knew. He was still caught in the nightmare, fighting to escape. Fighting to defend her. He'd helped her escape and was trying to keep them—

"A dream," she told herself, firmly. "Just a dream." But she couldn't shake the reality of the white place, with its many doors and aura of fear and pain. Slowly, she made herself crawl away from the bed. When she was a few feet away she managed to rise to her knees, then get to her feet. Behind her, Cage continued to moan. The sounds nearly wrenched her heart out.

"Not real," she reminded herself, though the words came through gritted teeth.

She looked at the door. It was real. For a moment she was absolutely terrified to approach it, afraid it would lead to the white corridor.

But that was only in the dream. This door would lead to freedom. He couldn't stop her. He was helpless, captive—frightened and alone.

She passed a hand across her forehead, dragging sweat-damp hair away from her face. "Only a dream."

"Josephine!"

She spun around at Cage's guttural shout, her body going tense. But he had only cried out in his sleep. He wasn't trying to stop her; he was a prisoner on the bed. He was lost in the nightmare.

I have to help him.

Jo shook her head hard, trying to toss the thought away. She turned back to the door, made herself concentrate on it. It was a plain wooden door, brown, not white. She reached out toward the doorknob. All she had to do was open the door and walk away. Cage wasn't going to wake up.

*He might never wake up. He'd been willing to
die for me.*

It was a strange thought, but she believed it.
Cage was a psychic, and he'd been caught in a
mental trap. She'd been caught in it with him,
but he'd found the way out for her, pushed her
back into the waking world. He'd stayed behind
so she could make her escape.

Jo closed her eyes and pressed her fingers to
her temples. What was she thinking? What was
the matter with her?

"Josephine!"

"Damn!"

She was going to regret this, wasn't she? But
she didn't regret turning around and going back
to the bed. She didn't regret being needed, knowing that there was something she could do.

Cage was lying flat on his back, his muscles
tense as marble. Kneeling on the edge of the mattress, she grabbed Cage by the shoulders and
shook. Her efforts barely moved him. She pinched
his upper arms, she prodded his chest. Nothing.

"Wake up!" she shouted as she shook him
again. She leaned close to his ear. "Wake up—
Marc. Marcus Cage, you wake up right this
minute!"

He moaned at the sound of his name and his
head turned toward her, so she shouted again.

"Marc!"

She patted his cheek, but the pat turned into a caress along his jawline. Then her fingers traced his lips. They were warm and soft. Touching them sent little shock waves along her fingertips and coiled heat deep inside her.

"Marc! Come on, wake up. It's Jo—Josephine."

"Josephine."

He whispered the word like a prayer. The sound made her shiver. And a feeling that was bright as fire, sharp as pain, stabbed her heart. The emotion the sound awoke in her was more complex than any she'd known before. It was—

"Josephine." Not a prayer this time, but a demand.

The sound sent fire racing through her. She stroked his cheeks, traced his lips again, ran her hands down his neck and across his wide shoulders. His body was so hard, the muscles perfectly molded, so very male. Just looking at him was an erotic experience; touching him was a joy.

"My Josephine," he said, and finally opened his eyes.

His deep voice set erotic vibrations all through her. Her head came up, and she was caught by his dark brown gaze for a long moment. Need and hunger blazed between them as they stared at each other. Her breath caught, and her heart lurched.

"You're awake," she managed to say, though her voice was thick with desire. Fierce hunger set her head reeling. She gazed at his face, at his beautiful eyes, and full, sensuous lips, and wanted as she'd never wanted before.

The back of his hand came up to brush across her cheek. "Don't cry."

She wasn't crying, or if she was, it didn't matter. It wasn't because he was lost and hurting and she was scared of losing him. It was because she'd found him, or because she was finding something in herself. If she was crying, it was because she'd never felt anything so, so—*this*—before. Whatever it was. The only place it was, was in this bed, with him.

"I'm here." He drew her to him, holding on to her like a lifeline.

Maybe she was crying, because she was blind all of a sudden. Everything went blurry, like a heat haze coming up off a wildfire. All she had were her other senses, and they were demanding touch and smell and taste.

She touched her lips to his, all fear of him was lost. Kissing him was more necessary than breathing. More necessary than sanity. More necessary than right or wrong, good or bad.

No names, no history, no future. Just them. This bed. Now.

There was nothing gentle or tentative in her kiss; it was passionate and insistent. *Mine!* She thought.

Yes. Yours, was his response.

While their mouths were still locked together, in one swift movement she was suddenly on her back. The swift shift made her dizzy, like a feather in a hurricane. Or maybe it was the kiss, which made her head spin, made her drunk with desire. She reveled in the sensation.

She moaned in protest when his head came up, then gasped in pleasure when he bent over her again and took one of her stiff nipples into his mouth, sending a sweet ache through her.

Her hand landed on the back of his shaved skull and pressed his head back down to her breast. The breath from his silent laughter tickled her flesh. He suckled and teased her nipple, and brought his hand up to fondle her other breast. He nuzzled her, and gently scraped the tips of fangs over her skin. His mouth throbbed, wanting to bite down, but he kept the impulse at bay. Instead he made love to her man to woman, taking pleasure in giving simple, uncomplicated human pleasure.

He took his time, moving from one spot on

Josephine's slender body to the next, learning her scents, her curves and hollows, what merely pleased her, and what drove her arousal higher. He kissed his way down her belly and between her thighs. His tongue found her swollen clitoris and brought her to a quick, hard orgasm. Her taste was a salty-sweet triumph to him as he worked his way back up her body. She moaned and writhed against him, alive with need, her hunger growing rather than being sated.

The more he caressed her, the more sounds of pleasure she made, the more she responded to his touch, the further he was drawn out of the hellish dream. She brought him back to life, away from the dark edge of oblivion. She made him hard as hell, made his fangs throb and his cock throb. He wanted to be inside her, but he didn't allow himself that pleasure yet. He wanted to savor Josephine for as long as she wanted him to make love to her. All her need poured into him, filled his mind, fired his body. What she needed, he needed. The need brought them together, body and soul.

The bond was beginning.

The realization made him happy, and he smiled. She gazed back but her eyes were huge with desire, unfocused, her expression completely rapt. If a bit of fang pressed over his lips, she didn't notice.

She lifted a hand toward him. "What— don't—"

"Stop? All right." He began to caress her again.

Her breasts were firm and very sensitive. He wanted to spend a lifetime touching, tasting, and teasing them. When he moved down, he found the scars along her ribs and across her belly. He kissed them and stroked them, letting her know that every inch of her body was beautiful. He told her so, whispering against her skin.

"You survived," he told her. "You're a survivor. You're strong."

Jo marveled at his tenderness, marveled at how it aroused her far more than any other words ever had.

"Even when these are gone"—he kissed the scars one by one again, moving deliberately down her body—"I will honor them. Love them."

This moved her too much. "Hush," she said. Lust was enough for her right now.

She ran her hands over his back and shoulders, stroked down his chest and the hard, rippling muscles of his abdomen. "Damn, you're hot."

"Don't swear, it's not becoming in a lady."

She laughed. His ability to make her laugh was as much a turn-on as everything else about him.

Somehow he made her whole; this stranger in her bed had become her whole world. She wanted this man and intended to appreciate him to the utmost. She was glad the light was on so she could see what she touched, what she claimed.

She ran her hands down the length of his back, traced his narrow waist and cupped his buttocks, before moving around to stroke his hips and the fronts of his bulging thighs.

She leaned her face close to his throat and drank in his musky, masculine scent. "Cage, you're amazing."

"You have yet to—oh!"

She'd reached the thick length of penis that jutted up between them. She stroked him from base to tip and back down. It was hot and heavy in her hand, as beautifully formed as the rest of him. His hips jerked, then he deliberately stilled at her touch, moaned.

"There is so much of you, Cage."

"No more than you can handle." He scooped her up and laid her down beneath him.

Her legs came up and open, her hips rose to meet him even as he pulled her forward. He entered her slowly, filled her. She was tight and wet and more than ready for him.

"More," she whispered, pleaded.

But he took his time, took her higher with long, slow strokes that filled her, excited her, made her beg for—

"More!" she demanded, and wrapped her legs around his waist. She ground against him, pulled him to her, as deep into her as he could go.

He groaned finally, and gave in to their mutual need. She threw her head back and rode out the building storm. When they came, it was together. Not just joined bodies reaching a blinding climax in an explosive instant. They were completely intertwined, ecstasy multiplied, blending, spiraling out of control as one.

Jo was outside herself for a long time, soaring, flying with Cage in some glorious place where she was not alone and where she never wanted to come down. But gradually her spirit sank back into her body, a body that was weak from the pleasure, where small aftershock orgasms rippled through her, keeping her insides quivering and her body singing.

Cage had collapsed on top of her, slick with sweat. His weight anchored her back into the world, back on the bed, and reality slowly took hold of her again. It grew harder and harder to keep her eyes open. Would she dream if she fell asleep? She wondered if the nightmare would return or if their sleep would be deep and peaceful.

"Oh, screw it," she muttered.

"Language," Cage murmured and was asleep as soon as he spoke.

She barely had time to be surprised as he took her with him into deep, delicious oblivion.

Chapter Fifteen

"Good morning, do we have any Oreos left?" Josephine asked as he rolled over to let her slip out of bed.

He'd been awake for a while but had enjoyed holding her as she slept utterly relaxed in his arms. He'd always thought he wasn't sentimental, but for a few minutes he imagined doing this every night for the rest of his long life.

When she finally stirred, he greeted her with a lengthy kiss that she returned with enthusiasm. But before he could take it any further, she grew distracted. He sensed hunger in her even before she was aware that she needed to eat, and he reluctantly let her go. Mortals just didn't have any stamina, at least at the beginning of a relationship.

"You don't need chocolate," Marc answered. He'd noticed that she said *we,* and wondered if she did. "You have me."

"Sex is not a substitute for chocolate," she answered. "Chocolate is not a substitute for sex. A woman needs a balance of both in her life."

He propped himself up against the pillows and put his hands behind his head. Her bare back was to him as she stood by the dresser where he'd piled their few possessions. "You look beautiful this evening," he said. "I like a naked woman, even when she's rummaging through a grocery bag for crumbs."

"You look eminently smug and satisfied this evening," she answered.

"I have good reason."

Jo turned and looked at Cage. He was stretched out in the middle of the bed like a potentate waiting to be entertained by his harem. Or, an analogy more to her liking, he looked like dessert. No, the main course of a very rich banquet, as sculpted by Michelangelo. She'd found the cookie bag and made a production of taking an Oreo apart and licking up the sweet filling while she let her gaze drift over the naked Mr. Cage. He was a big, powerfully built man in the prime of life, and she enjoyed the way just looking at him sent flashes of heat through her. She hadn't felt so alive, so sensually female, for a very long time.

"Prime," she said, remembering hearing him call himself that. The man from the couple they'd rescued had used the word as well, used it like a title. "Prime," she repeated.

Cage looked curiously at her. "Yes?"

"What's a prime?"

"I am. A Prime is a fully sexually mature male in control of his powers, a male who accepts responsibility for his actions, and responsibility for the safety, comfort, and happiness of those he takes under his protection."

"I—see."

He shook his head. "No, you don't. But someday the explanation will make sense to you, I promise."

Jo's stomach rumbled, and she ate another cookie while trying to puzzle through what Cage meant. After she swallowed, she asked, "So, Primes—like you—are people who live by a code of honor?"

"More like a code of tradition." He shrugged. "Works for our cultures."

"Cultures?"

"You're lucky I'm Family, because the rules for being Prime are even more complicated for the Clan boys, and the Tribe Primes don't follow any rules."

She wished she hadn't brought the subject up, as his explanations were making her nervous. She'd gone for hours thinking he was sane— why? Because he was good in bed?—and now he was telling her about arcane and strange rules for some underground society he was part of.

He couldn't have made the whole thing up since he wasn't the only one who'd used the term. Of course, the naked guy and his pregnant wife had been pretty strange, too.

"Who were those people?" she asked. "Did you know them?"

"What people?"

"Oh, as if I've had so much contact with crowds since we ran into each other. The couple you rescued, of course."

Cage rubbed his jaw, then the back of his neck. "If I tell you, you won't believe me."

She put her hands on her hips, and he suddenly grinned. His expression made her realize how much he was enjoying her nakedness, and all of a sudden her nipples stiffened, and moist heat flared between her legs.

She refused to give in to this sudden arousal, and continued to glare at him. "Try me." He started to get up off the bed to come to her, but she held up a hand and insisted, "Tell me about those people."

He sat on the edge of the bed. "I didn't know them personally, but I recognized what they are. They aren't the same as my people; but they are psychics, with different types of gifts." He rubbed the back of his neck again. "You're psychic," he reminded her. "I found you because I sensed your presence. Like calls to like. That's the most logical explanation I can give you."

"What's the illogical one?"

"You mean the truth?" He gave her a long, hard stare. "They're werefoxes."

"They were foxes?"

"Oh, no, you heard me right. Don't try to pretend you didn't."

She wished she hadn't insisted on an answer. Why couldn't she leave well enough alone and pretend that the man who'd kidnapped her wasn't crazy? And, by the way, she reminded herself, he *had* kidnapped her. She shouldn't forget that just because she'd made love to him. And wanted to make love to him again.

He was psychic, she had to give him that.

She suddenly felt tired and depressed. She wanted some privacy. "Can I take a shower? By myself?"

He looked disappointed. "Sure," he answered gruffly. "There's no window in the bathroom."

Cage certainly wasn't forgetting about their captor/captive relationship, even if she'd crossed the line when she had sex with him. "If I were going to escape, I could have done it last night," she snapped.

Stung by her bitterness, Marc came to his feet and stalked across the room to her. He hated the way Josephine flinched slightly at his approach, but she stood her ground. He tried very hard not to loom over her and kept his voice gentle. "What do you mean you could have escaped? Why didn't you? When was this?"

She blushed and looked away.

"Josephine," he insisted. Then he caught a flash of memory as it leapt through her mind. A memory that belonged to him, as well.

They ran, barely keeping their footing on the blood-slick floor. Without looking back they knew the guards were there, gaining on them with every step. They weren't going to escape.

He'd almost forgotten the dream; making love to her had flushed that horror out of his mind. It rushed back now with enough force to twist his stomach with fear. He went cold, as cold as he'd been running down that long, white hallway with Josephine at his side. That was wrong. She shouldn't have been there. Had it been a dream or a premonition?

He was confused for a moment, forgetting what they'd been talking about as the world around him spun out of what little control he thought he'd won back. Then he said firmly, trying to make himself believe it, "It was only a dream."

"It—was worse than a dream."

"You were in the lab. With me. They caught you, too." He pulled her into a tight embrace, wanting to put himself between her and any harm.

"I couldn't leave you." She spoke with her lips against his shoulder. The words were garbled, but he understood her meaning. "I couldn't leave you trapped there."

He remembered that they ran and ran, then they'd reached an open door. He'd pushed her through it, then turned to face their captors. She must have woken up. He must have stayed inside the nightmare.

"It was only a dream," he said. He ran his fingers through her short hair. She'd begun to quietly sob. "Only a dream," he promised. "Don't let it upset you anymore."

She lifted her head, and her eyes shone with tears and anger. "You were trapped! I couldn't leave you. I thought you were going to die in there. I went back for you." She blinked, and moisture glittered like crystals on her lashes. "Was that stupid, or what?" she asked.

"It was a nightmare," he said. "A bad one, but it was a dream." He was grateful for her concern, for her caring. He wanted to lie to her and tell her that she'd saved his life, but he couldn't. "I would have woken up eventually."

"So I should have just left you to sleep it off?" He nodded. "Damn."

She tried to pull away from him, but he held her gently in his grasp. "Josephine, what have I told you about that kind of language?"

She wasn't amused. "Let me go," she demanded.

He knew she was embarrassed now, and feeling like a fool. He hated having her feel like that. "Listen," he said, "your instincts are good, and your reaction's understandable. You were shaken by a very, very bad dream, a dream that you did share with me. There was telepathy involved, and your own special kind of empathy, and your own bad memories and what I've put you through kicked into the mix. That's a pretty weird combination. The weirdness didn't disappear immediately when you came to consciousness. You were still partly caught in the dream. You believed in the reality of it."

"Damn right I did. I was *there.*"

"So instead of walking out the door like the smart woman you are, you did what you could to help me."

"But you said it was only a dream."

"Yeah, but neither of us believed it at the time. I was lost in the weirdness, too. So . . ." He kissed her forehead, then tilted her chin up so he could gently brush his lips across hers. "Thank you, Josephine."

She still needed some space and time to deal with her feelings on her own, so Marc reluctantly took a step back. "Go take your shower."

She grabbed some things out of her bag and fled into the other room. Marc stood very still, watching the closed bathroom door until he heard the shower start. Then he got dressed and began to pace the room restlessly.

Good goddess, what had he done? The dream was a warning, wasn't it? He hadn't been able to think clearly those first few nights, hadn't had the strength to make any decision not related to his survival.

But there came a time in every Prime's life when he could no longer just look out for number one. He'd taken Josephine under his protection; he was responsible for her. Had he told her that? He couldn't remember. It wasn't formal until the words were spoken.

He had told her she belonged to him, though, and that was enough. The Matri, his great-grandmother, matriarch of the Caeg Family, would certainly rule that he'd made a bondmate commitment to the mortal woman Josephine Elliot.

Rights and responsibilities aside, he'd gotten her into this; it was time he got her out.

He felt like he'd been running in circles when he needed to be running as fast and far as he could away from danger. And didn't think he'd gotten very far from where he'd started. If it hadn't been for the wildfires, and the foxes, and Josephine's reasonable insistence on escape attempts that left him enervated, he could have made some progress by now.

He had to run fast and hard away from Arizona now to make up time. If not home, maybe he should go to one of the Clan citadels up north. If the foxes had gotten his message out, the Clans would all be up in arms by now. They'd be willing to mount a crusade, and he'd be happy to ally with them.

Those hunting him had all the resources, a cunning leader, and believed the prize was the secret of immortality. All he had was himself, and Josephine.

Soon he wouldn't have her. Not until he could come back and claim her safely.

He was already missing her when she came out of the bathroom. For a moment he sat on the bed and looked at her, memorizing her. Her hair was wet and slicked back off her face. She looked warily back at him, a slender woman in khaki shorts and a T-shirt with a Union Jack flag outlining her breasts. He was aware of how vulnerable she was, and it fueled the need to protect her.

"What?" she finally asked, breaking the silence.

Marc stood, tossed what was left of her cash on the bed, and walked to the door. He wasn't going to take her in his arms and kiss her good-bye. He'd find her when he could. Even without the beginning of a bond, he knew he could find her.

"Time to leave," he said. He held one of her sets of keys in his hand.

She looked from the money to him, totally confused. "Is that a major tip for the maid?"

"It's for you. Sit down," he added. He waited until she had before he went on. "Believe me when I tell you it's safer not to go to the authorities. To explain why you've been missing so long, tell them your car broke down and you had to hike around the fires. Tell them whatever you want." He gave her another long, hard look. He almost apologized for what he'd done to her. Instead, he said, "Stay safe, Josephine. Go home."

Then he did the hardest thing he'd ever done. He opened the door and walked away, leaving the woman he loved behind.

Chapter Sixteen

For a very brief moment, Jo almost acted on the insane impulse to run after him and beg him to take her with him. She was not crazy, though. She did not throw away the opportunity he'd given her to have her life back. But she didn't know what to do, either.

So she sat unmoving on the edge of the bed, her hands clasped tightly on her lap. For a long time she was numb, empty, full of dozens of conflicting emotions but no coherent thoughts.

She finally became aware of how empty the room was, how *alone* she was. Cage had an overwhelming, dominant presence. Without him there, the world was silent. She was alone in the room, alone inside her head. His emotions had bombarded her for days, keeping her constantly off-balance. She'd had to fight against his will, fight against sympathizing with him, fight against his crazy claims, fight caring for him, and fight and lose to a growing sexual attraction. She'd fought fear, and she'd fought uncertainty. What was she supposed to do with nothing to fight anymore?

She was free. The realization came slowly; but it came with no joy, no victory, no pleasure. There was relief at being alive, but she'd stopped believing he was going to kill her the night he rescued the—the foxlike people.

She shook her head, and realized her muscles were stiff. How long had she been sitting here? Where was he? Where had he gone?

Would he be all right?

Then her deep worry for him was replaced with the outraged thought, *He stole my Jeep!*

Her anger pumped enough adrenaline into her system to get her on her feet and make her finally, truly aware that she could go anywhere she wanted, do anything she wanted. Marc Cage wasn't lurking out in the hall ready to jump at her if she opened the door and tell her that her freedom was a practical joke.

No. There was a part of her that was aware of him moving away from her, a connection between them that tugged on her heart.

She shook her head again, trying to deny any psychic link. "Stop that. That's nonsense. Mumbo jumbo."

To keep from thinking about the mumbo jumbo that she more than half believed, Jo looked around. He'd managed to find them another motel room without a phone or television. The man had a gift for finding really out-of-the-way places in the middle of nowhere. "If you want a real secluded getaway, let Marcus Cage book the tour for you," she muttered.

Getting away had been the point, of course. She still didn't know who he'd been running from, or why.

But the point is, she told herself, *you aren't running from anyone. Get out of here and find a phone.*

Should she call the cops? Yeah. One cop. Her mom. Her family had to be frantic by now.

Jo stuffed the cash in her pocket, and went to the door. Turning the knob proved to be hard. Walking out into the hallway was harder. By the time she stood in the center of the narrow motel corridor, she was furious with Cage for breeding this trepidation in her. It didn't help that the hall reminded her of the dream.

At least Cage wasn't waiting for her. And this time no one chased her as she walked, then ran toward the door at the end of the corridor. When she reached the door she banged into it so hard she bruised her shoulder in her haste to get out.

She forgot the pain the instant she stepped out under the open night sky; she looked around and saw lots of parked vehicles, a few people going about their business, and a scattering of buildings. She soaked in the sights and sounds as she turned around and around. The night air was cool on her skin. She heard a train in the far distance. A truck horn blasted the quiet evening air as a huge eighteen-wheeler sped past the motel. The stink of its exhaust filled her lungs.

"Ah, civilization."

Cage had left her in a small town, though she had no idea where. It didn't matter. He hadn't abandoned her to fend for herself in the middle of nowhere. She wasn't a prisoner; she could do what she wanted.

She spotted a restaurant across the street and decided to go have a salad. She was suddenly determined that the first thing she was going to reclaim about her life was being a vegetarian.

Actually, the very first thing she did when she walked into the restaurant was to use the pay phone by the cashier station to dial a collect call.

"Yes, Mom, it's Josephine," she said when she finally got through.

"Josephine?" her mom asked, sounding almost skeptical. "Josephine? Is that really you?"

What was wrong? Jo was hurt until she

remembered that she hadn't let anyone call her by her full name since she was twelve. Her mother worked missing persons cases, and knew all the tricks the media, creeps, and crazies used to get at victims' families. No wonder she was suspicious.

"It's really Jo, Mom. Really. I'm fine."

"Oh, my God!" her mother shouted. "Oh, my God! You're alive! Sweetheart, we were so worried." Then Constance Elliot switched from mother mode to detective lieutenant mode. "Where are you? What happened? Can you talk?"

Jo looked at the woman behind the cash register and asked the name of the town. The woman looked surprised, but told her. "Kennedyville, Mom. I—" She wasn't used to lying to anyone, especially to her parents. "I got lost. The Jeep broke down, and I had to hike around the fires."

"Really?" The skeptical tone had returned. "Kennedyville, you say?"

"Yes."

"Fine. You stay right there. I'll call the local sheriff—"

"No!" Jo interrupted. "No police, please."

"And why the devil not? You're a missing person. There's a very intense search going on for you."

"I'm sure there is, and I'm grateful. But I'm not lost, I'm found. I'm fine. Really. I don't want any attention."

"Jo, are you sure you're safe?"

"Yes." The cashier was staring at her, and Jo turned her back to the woman. She whispered, putting her hand up to muffle the conversation further as she gave an excuse that her very sharp mother would believe. "I can't stand any more media attention. Remember what it was like after the crash? I can't go through that again. They'll drag up my past."

"They already have. You obviously haven't caught any news broadcasts."

"No, and I don't want to. Mom, please, keep this quiet. Just come and get me, okay?"

She really didn't want to have to face the media again. The spotlight that had been turned on the pilot who'd survived had been agonizing. It had been hard enough being hailed a hero. She feared that a flimsy story of her getting lost wouldn't hold up if reporters decided to look into it.

"Just come get me," she pleaded. "Let the family know I'm okay, tell them I love them, and come get me." She didn't wait for an answer, but hung up the phone. She wiped a hand across her stinging eyes. Damn, she was crying again.

Language, Josephine.

I'll swear inside my head if I want to.

She had to be imagining Cage talking in her head. She was just tired and very stressed out. Maybe she'd have that salad, give herself time to get her thoughts together, then call home again.

Beyond the cash register, there was a row of booths and a lunch counter with a half dozen stools. The kitchen was visible beyond the counter, and the smell of coffee and deep-fried food wafted through the air. The food smelled good, and she stood and breathed in the scents for a moment.

The cashier was looking at her worriedly. "You all right, honey?" she asked. "You a refugee from the fire, too?"

Jo remembered how full the motel lot was, and she finally noticed that the restaurant was crowded. Refugees from the wildfire? Of course. Many of these people must have lost their homes, or been evacuated by firefighters. She knew that drill. She'd helicoptered people out of harm's way herself in years past. Other people had been caught up in their own emergencies while she was isolated in Cage's company.

She nodded to the cashier. "Yes. Can I get something to eat?"

The woman pointed to an empty stool at the counter. "Have a seat."

When Jo sat down and picked up a menu, she found herself missing Cage. And she found the quiet of the place disconcerting, as well. It wasn't that no one was talking; there were conversations going on all around her. A baby was crying in one of the booths. There was the clink and clatter of dishes and flatware, the hum of air-conditioning, and sounds of cooking from the kitchen. The type of quiet Jo was suddenly aware of was something she'd never experienced before as an empath. It was an emotional quiet, an absence of perception. One of her senses was suddenly missing. She couldn't feel them. She'd been empathic all her life. She'd learned to control it and done just fine. After the accident she'd felt too much, she'd been bombarded, overwhelmed. She had been drowning before meeting Cage, so soaked and saturated with others' emotions that running away from the world had been her only option. She'd yearned for the silence.

It was silent, and she had only her own thoughts and feelings to deal with. Was this what it was like to be normal? She wasn't sure if she liked the isolation or not.

Don't worry about it; it's probably a reaction

from spending so much time with Cage. Maybe concentrating so intently on one person fried whatever brain circuit controls the empathy.

Her empathic gift would either come back, or it wouldn't. It wouldn't do any harm for her simply to be normal for a while. Normal was good. Normal didn't get people into trouble. She wasn't going to let herself worry about psychic stuff when she needed to concentrate on getting home and getting day-to-day life back on track.

"You ready?" the waitress asked.

Jo looked up. "Scrambled eggs," she said, suddenly not wanting a salad after all. "And toast with lots of butter and jelly, and hash browns, and maybe some pancakes."

"You want any sausage?"

"Yes." The answer surprised Jo, but she didn't retract it. "Just pile a lot of cholesterol on a plate, and I'll eat it." Cage would be proud.

The waitress laughed. "You sound like you've been lost out in the desert for a month."

"More like a couple of weeks," Jo said. "And I'd like coffee and orange juice, too, please."

It wasn't as if Cage had starved her, she thought, as the waitress turned away. Far from it, he'd been worried that she was skinny. That was rather sweet—except for the kidnapping part.

Don't romanticize him. Just don't. And don't

sit here half in tears from missing him. That's too weird.

Her coffee and juice arrived, and she concentrated on them. When several large plates of food arrived, she was able to focus on the meal. There was a lot of food, and Jo took a long time eating it. She slowly worked her way through everything she'd ordered, happily accepting frequent refills of coffee.

For all she knew, hours had passed by the time a hand landed on her shoulder, and she looked up into a stranger's face. The man was in his late forties, with buzz-cut steel gray hair and bags under his eyes. He wore a police uniform.

"Jo Elliot?" he asked.

Not so long ago, the sight of a cop would have thrilled her, now all it did was annoy her. Hadn't she asked to be left alone? "Did my mother call you?"

A flicker of surprise crossed his features, but he calmly answered, "Our office was contacted by Lieutenant Elliot."

The restaurant was silent, with everyone watching. Jo hated the attention. "Thank you for your concern," she said quietly. "I'm fine, and I'm sorry for the inconvenience. I'm waiting for my family to come get me, so—"

"Your mother asked me to bring you to the

office," he interrupted. The hand on her shoulder subtly urged her to stand. "You can wait for her there. That's where she'll be expecting to find you," he added, when Jo looked around the restaurant uncertainly.

It was true that she hadn't told her mother where to pick her up. The police station would offer more privacy than waiting here. Now that there'd been attention drawn to her, the last thing she wanted was more. She didn't want anything to do with the authorities. Marc had asked her not to go to them. Well, they'd come to her. Not because of him, they didn't know about her connection to him.

She overheard someone in the crowd say, "I think I saw her picture on the news channel. Isn't she the one lost in the fire zone?"

"I think so," someone else said.

This recognition from a stranger tipped the balance in favor of going with the officer even more than the fact that he had his hand on her arm and didn't look like he was going anywhere. "I'll wait at the police station," she told him. She paid for her meal and accompanied him to his car.

There was no conversation on the way to the small cinder-block building. Once inside, she was shown to a room with bare walls that held only a table and two chairs. She was told to have a seat, then left alone. For a while she was glad of the privacy, but as time passed she grew restless, and the silence and isolation began to wear on her nerves. When she got up and tried the door, she discovered that it was locked. She went to the window, but it was small and set high in the wall. There was no seeing out, and no getting out, as it was barred.

Nervousness turned to a sense of dread, which edged into fear. She tried shouting and banging on the door, but no one paid any attention. She paced around and around the table for a long time, but eventually sat back down.

She must have fallen asleep because her head was resting on the table when the door opened. She bolted to her feet as a man came into the room. She had to blink to bring him into focus. He was tall and handsome, with a cleft chin, blue eyes, and short blond hair. He was wearing a suit and carrying a leather case. There was a look about him that said "cop" to the cop's daughter, but not just any kind of cop. FBI, maybe. Something federal.

"Who are you?" she demanded. "Why am I being held here?"

"Sit down, Ms. Elliot," he said smoothly, with a smile and a gesture toward her chair. He closed the door behind him and crossed the room to take the chair opposite her. "I'm sorry to have left you waiting so long."

He folded his hands on the table and looked at her, very calm, very professional. He watched her for a few seconds, then he said, "I need you to tell me where to find Marcus Cage."

Chapter Seventeen

She'd already been expecting the question. She chose to ignore it.

She said, "I've had a rough few days. I'm very tired, and I want to go home to my family."

"I understand that," he replied. "I sympathize with your ordeal, and I don't want to add to the trauma any more than necessary. But I still need information from you." He took a leather wallet out of his jacket. "My name is Jonas Gavin," he said as he handed her the case. He sat back in his chair and waited while she flipped it open and studied the badge and identification card inside.

She'd been right about his being from a federal agency, but the FBI guess was incorrect. "Special Agent Gavin," she said, and passed the ID back to him. She didn't know what else to say.

"Call me Gavin," he said. "Most people do." He tucked the badge away and folded his hands again. His movements were deliberately calm and nonthreatening, and all she had was body language to tell what he was feeling, since her gift of empathy was gone. He turned a sympathetic expression on her. "Cage has put you through a lot, but it's safe for you to talk about him now."

The last thing Jo wanted to do was talk about Cage, and certainly not to this stranger. She didn't even want to think about Cage. She'd started her trip into the desert confused, despondent, and in physical as well as mental pain. Truth be told, she'd run off to feel sorry for herself in private.

All she wanted was to go home and take her life back. If Marcus Cage had done nothing else for her, he'd shown her how precious home, family, and freedom were. He'd even given her some good advice and tried to make her face some of her fears. She owed him for shaking her out of her self-pitying depression.

"Marcus Cage," Gavin said.

Jo realized she'd been staring at the wall and had almost forgotten the man was there. She looked at him and wondered how she was going to get past him. She didn't know what to say. She didn't want to lie, and she wasn't very good at it, anyway. It would be annoying and ironic if Cage gave her freedom, but she didn't get a chance to use it because of him.

Then again, she didn't *have* to talk to Gavin, did she? The fact that she'd been locked in this room was ominous, but it had probably been mistaken zealousness on the part of local cops who'd been under orders to hold her until this federal type showed up.

She stood, and said, "I'm sorry your time has been wasted, but I'm not going to be any help to you."

Gavin let her get almost to the door before he said, "Your trying to buy him time won't help him. I think you want to help him." She heard him push back his chair and stand. "He's going to die if you don't help him."

Jo halted in front of the door as Gavin's words sent a chill up her spine. She stood frozen, shoulders hunched as though waiting for a blow. Guilt raced through her as she remembered the people who'd died in the crash. She hadn't been able to help them. She had a sudden image of Cage hurt and dying, and it terrified her.

But Cage was alive—free. Running. She didn't know what he was running from, she didn't know where he was going, but she wasn't going to let anyone try to stop him.

Why?

She forced the question away, took another step toward the door.

"If you walk away from this, he'll die."

She desperately wanted to run, but Gavin's calm certainty drew her back. She turned to face him.

"I want to help him, too," he said, when she looked at him. "I can't help him if I can't find him. You hold the key to that."

"I don't," she said, having at least that much truth to share with the agent. She shook her head. "I really don't."

"There are tears in your eyes," Gavin told her. "Don't tell me you don't know who I'm talking about."

"I'm not telling you anything," she snapped back. She forced herself to add, more calmly, "I've been out in the desert, lost near the fires. I don't know why you make assumptions about me. All I want is to go home." She turned around.

"The door's locked," Gavin said, before she reached it. "I know you're tired, but I can't let you go until you help me."

She spun back around. "Are you charging me with a crime? Do I need to call a lawyer?"

"A lawyer won't do you any good," he said. "Not with the kind of power my agency wields."

He held his hands up before him. "But I'm not here to threaten you. I'm trying to make this easy on you."

He was so very calm, so neatly groomed, well dressed, polite, and totally in control. It looked like she'd traded one captor for another. And frankly, she preferred big, gruff, grubby Marcus Cage to the slick Mr. Gavin.

"You are threatening me," she told Gavin. "Locking me in this room is a threat."

He nodded. "You're correct, of course, but I need your cooperation. I need it quickly. Please believe that talking to me is for the best. I won't force anything on you. I won't hurt you. Terrorize you." After a long pause that left her enough time to go cold with dread knowing what was coming, he added, "Rape you."

The words still felt like a blow, no matter how neutral the man's tone. "I haven't been raped," she answered, making herself look Gavin in the eye.

"You're sure?"

She didn't offer any more comment despite the look of concern in his eyes. She wished she hadn't even answered him; it was none of his business. What had happened was no one's business but hers and Cage's.

She was cold, goose bumps dotted her skin; it

felt like the air-conditioning had been cranked up to stun. And the lights in this interrogation room were too bright. The walls were a dull beige, and it felt like they were closing in on her. She was deliberately being made to feel that cooperating with Gavin was the only way she was going to get out of here, wasn't she?

Or maybe she was being paranoid, and the man really was trying to be patient and as kind as possible under the circumstances.

And the circumstances were . . . ? Why was Cage running? Why were the feds chasing him? She'd been a pawn the whole time, kept in the dark, sometimes literally. What the hell was going on? She practically had to bite her tongue to keep from shouting the question at the special agent. If she gave in to curiosity now, it would be an admission that she knew Marcus Cage.

Gavin had put his briefcase next to his chair; now he picked it up and put it on the table. When he opened it he took out several items, among them her wallet and one of her Def Leppard T-shirts, as well as one of the white shirts Cage had worn.

"Our forensic team has been through the room where you and Cage stayed. There was evidence of sexual activity on the bed linens. We have a match for Cage's DNA, and I'm certain a sample of your DNA would show that you were his sexual partner." He'd been looking down as he spoke, now he raised his head to look at her sharply. "Are you sure it wasn't rape, Jo?"

"Of course, I—!" Jo clapped a hand over her mouth to keep from saying more.

She'd never been so mortified in her life, or felt so humiliated. It wasn't that she was ashamed of the sex, it was the clinical proof of its being presented to her by a stranger that was so awful. It made her feel as if she needed to justify her actions, as if she should apologize for making love to a man she'd wanted. Gavin was doing a good job of making her feel dirty, and that made her angry.

She'd made the choice to make love to Cage.

It might have been a reckless choice, but it had been the right one at that moment. What had happened between them was an act of fiery intensity and sweet fulfillment. She could almost still feel his body twined with hers, the perfect way they fit together, how they made each other whole. Just thinking about it made her ache to do it all over again.

"Mind your own business," she said to Gavin.

"Marcus is my business," he answered. He sat back in his chair. "I think you *think* you made love to him, Jo, but that isn't what really happened."

"I was there."

He shook his head. "Not really. Not exactly."

"You're about to bring up Stockholm Syndrome, aren't you?" she asked. "I know what it is; how hostages who spend long amounts of time in the company of their captors can come to identify with them. It's one of the things that helped me—"

She broke off again as she realized that she was telling Gavin things he wanted to know, that she had just admitted to being abducted and held prisoner.

"Being aware of a process doesn't mean that a person will be unaffected by it." Gavin leaned forward slightly, his gaze very intent on hers. "Shall I tell you what happened to you?"

"I know what happened to me."

"You were there when it happened, I know that. But you are too involved with the situation to understand it objectively. I can explain it to you."

Of course she wasn't objective about it! She hadn't even had time to think about it yet. Could a person ever be objective about an experience like that? Could she ever be anything but emotionally attached to Marc Cage? She felt like he was a part of her, that she was a part of him somehow.

"Jo." Gavin tapped a fingertip on the table to get her attention. "Jo," he repeated.

"What?"

"You were detached from the present, just then. Your thoughts were on Cage, weren't they?"

"Yes," she admitted.

"He's done that to you."

"Done what?" Why shouldn't she think about Cage?

"He's conditioned you to center your whole existence around him," Gavin told her. "He probably didn't even do it on purpose. Marcus is not the sort of person who'd deliberately set out to brainwash someone, but he would do anything he had to in his current condition to survive. He completely isolated you from the rest of the world," he went on. "Everything you did was completely under his control. What you ate and when, where you slept, where you went, how long you stayed, all at his discretion. Everything you had, he gave to you, every little privilege was his gift to you. That's all true, isn't it, Jo? What did he call you?" he added. "Josephine, perhaps?"

"Yes. How did you know—?"

"He took away your name and gave you one of his choosing. He needed to make you his, to make you feel like you belonged to him."

She wanted to protest that people who cared for each other gave each other nicknames, pet names. But a nagging voice spoke up inside her, questioning that perhaps Cage had given her a pet name was because he treated her like a pet. She *had* been dependant on him for everything, just like a puppy or a kitten. Or a prisoner.

He was a wanted man. He was on the run, with a government security agency hunting him. So he wasn't a garden variety criminal or prison escapee.

"Is he a terrorist?"

Gavin smiled. "No."

This answer came as a relief, though she didn't see why the agent found the question amusing. "What is Cage, then?" she demanded.

"Psychic," he said.

"You know about that?" she blurted out. "The government *believes* it?"

"Marcus Cage has a rare and dangerous gift."

"I thought he was a criminal!"

"He is, and an escapee. He is very dangerous in his current condition. Dangerous to others, and almost certainly fatally dangerous to himself if he isn't found soon. You have to help me find him. You have to help me for his sake, Jo. Never mind that he's a convicted criminal—"

"Convicted of what?" she interrupted. "Tell me he's not a murderer." *Please, not that. I can't bear it if he's a killer.* "He didn't hurt me," she added. "He let me go."

"He hasn't killed anyone, at least not yet. Despite his size and looks, he's not a violent offender. He was sentenced to three years in a minimum security facility for a white-collar crime."

Relief flooded her. He wasn't evil. She knew it in her gut, in her heart, but she was shaken enough by Gavin's descriptions of her captivity that she wasn't sure she could trust her instincts.

Then the incongruity struck her. "Wait a minute—if Cage isn't a dangerous criminal, and he escaped from a white-collar lockup, why the manhunt? Why are the feds involved?"

"There are things I can't tell you, Jo."

She laughed, and his evasiveness stiffened her resolve to have some control. She crossed her arms over her chest. "Then I guess there are a lot of things I can't tell you."

A flash of frustration cracked his calm veneer for the first time. "We don't have time for games."

"My life isn't a game. But you're playing games with me, setting boundaries for me. That's not acceptable. You drew me into this—"

"Cage dragged you into this."

"And I have a right to know what *this* is. What's going on? What's going to happen to him? Why is he—?" She took a deep breath before she added, "the way he is."

"Ah." Gavin nodded. "So you noticed."

"He's—not like other people," she said. "He—"

"Thinks he's a vampire."

"*What?*" She laughed. "Of course he doesn't—"

"Didn't he mention that to you? Didn't he tell you about his kind?"

"No. He talked about his family." A line of cold dread went up her spine, and she tried to shake the feeling off. "It sounded like they were from some secret ethnic minority."

"So he never said he was a vampire? In so many words?"

"No." she shook her head in disbelief.

"Didn't he bite you?"

Jo touched her throat, she looked at her wrist, she remembered a sting of pain and pleasure as Marc's mouth settled on her breast. "Yes, he bit me," she conceded. "But . . . he didn't mean anything by it. I suppose it's a fetish . . . a harmless turn-on and—"

"He drank your blood," Gavin cut off her rationalizing. "You don't want to remember it, or maybe he was able to use his telepathic gift to make you forget, or think it was something else. Believe it now, Jo. Cage drank your blood."

"Eeuwww!" She balked at this, totally disgusted. But she recalled how weak she'd been after that first night in the desert—how he'd come out of the dark like a nightmare come to life. He'd completely overwhelmed her, and—She touched her neck again. "He never said he's a vampire."

"What did he say?"

"That he wasn't mortal," she admitted. "That he was around eighty years old. That he'd escaped from people who were doing experiments on him. There were dreams," she added. "Horrible dreams."

Excitement burned in Gavin's eyes. "You shared his dreams?"

"Yes. I know that sounds crazy."

It didn't *feel* crazy, not with the way she still felt connected, mind to mind, with Cage. Or maybe it was soul to soul. She had a moment of absurd humor, thinking that maybe she'd truly met her soul mate in Marcus Cage, and it turned out he really was an insane criminal. Wouldn't that be just—typical?

"It doesn't sound crazy to me, Jo." Gavin sounded very, very reassuring.

And Jo very much needed to be reassured. "Why isn't it crazy? There's no such thing as a vampire, so why did he bite me?"

"It's all related." Gavin looked at her for a few seconds, then shuffled his papers and tapped his fingertip on the table. Finally, he came to a decision, and looked at her again. "You are owed an explanation. Nothing I say leaves this room. Agreed?"

"Of course." She knew very well that if she didn't agree, she wouldn't find out anything. And she very much wanted to know everything she could about Marcus Cage.

He hesitated a moment longer, then said, "Marc volunteered for an experimental government program. Volunteered: be very clear on that. He was nearing the end of his prison sentence when he found out about the experimental program. He didn't do it to shorten his time. He went into it with his eyes open. He knew he was physically strong, and he was aware of his mental abilities, and was curious to see if he could take them further. The purpose of the program was to enhance both."

"Enhance? How?"

"With new types of drugs, new surgical procedures, new microtechnology." He smiled. "Remember the opening of the old television show, *The Six Million Dollar Man?*"

She did, and nodded.

"The price of the work has been a lot closer to six billion."

"But why do these *enhancements* to Marc?"

It was a stupid question. One she knew the answer to even as he said, "There have been science-fiction stories about building supersoldiers for a long time, but this program is the real deal—or will be, if the techniques are perfected. If not, if we can't correct the psychoses the experimental drugs have produced in the volunteers, then the program will be shut down. We set out to enhance Marcus Cage and succeeded to a certain degree. Are you following me?"

"You were trying to make Superman?"

Gavin nodded.

This explanation, bizarre as it seemed, made a lot more sense than Cage's being a vampire. "And you run these experiments out of Area 51, right?" Everybody knew about the supersecret government experimental base in the Nevada desert, but nobody knew what went on there.

"Are you taking me seriously, Jo? Because Marc's life is at stake."

She recalled how Cage had been able to read her mind, to hypnotize her almost at will. She supposed that drugs could have been developed to up the abilities of someone who was already psychic. She remembered how his eyes seemed to glow red sometimes. Was that some sort of night-vision device surgically implanted in his eyes? She remembered how he'd outrun the Jeep when she tried to escape. Enhanced muscles and cardiovascular system? She remembered how he was sensitive to light. Was that a drug reaction?

"Have the drugs you've given him made him delusional?" she asked Gavin.

"Exactly," he answered. "His mind has created a detailed fantasy world where he believes himself to be a vampire. There are things we did to him that reinforce this belief. The drugs have given him a serious reaction to sunlight. He does crave blood. Again, the drugs did that to him. We are responsible for what's wrong with him, and we want to help him."

"He's an experiment gone wrong, enhanced with a lot of classified technology." Jo found it hard to believe that the people who created Cage were only looking out for his good. "That's why you want him back?"

"He's also an escaped prisoner, one with paranoid delusions that are only going to get worse," Gavin answered. "He's getting more dangerous all the time. You were the first person he took hostage, and he let you go. But he's going to reach a point where he can't let go, where he's going to drain an innocent victim's blood, and somebody is going to get killed. He won't be able to help himself. We really do want to help him," Gavin added. "I know you do, too."

He looked and sounded very sure, very earnest, and what he said shook her deeply. She sat and thought for a while. Gavin kept quiet and let her. She twisted her fingers together nervously in her lap, trying to decide whether to trust her heart or her head. Her heart said Marc had told her the truth. But the only element that Gavin's story didn't explain better were the things the werefox had said.

She looked up. "What's a Prime?"

"It's a term convicts use," Gavin answered. "It means an alpha male."

"Oh."

So, maybe the werefox wasn't a shapeshifting human after all. What was he, then? An ex-con who recognized Cage from prison? It made a hell of a lot more sense than tales of vampires and werecreatures. And Cage *was* sick. The drugs were driving him crazy. They might kill him.

She looked up again. "Can you save his life?"

"We want to try. We need your help. You can save him, Jo."

"How?"

"Lead us to him."

"How?" she asked again.

"You're connected, aren't you? Don't you feel it? The way you're protecting him convinces me that you're more than emotionally connected to him."

"I thought you said it was brainwashing?"

"Part of it was brainwashing, but not all. You spent days together, days full of intense emotional contact. He got inside your mind and under your skin psychically, along with messing with your head psychologically."

"Yes," she admitted. "We-we—" She couldn't explain it.

Gavin did it for her. "Experiments have proven that prolonged telepathic contact, especially between sexual partners, creates bonds between the partners. If you think about it very hard, you'll find the link between you. That link can lead you to him."

He sounded completely certain. She wasn't at all sure.

"Search inside yourself," he urged.

"Use the Force," she muttered.

He chuckled. "Call it whatever you want to."

Jo thought about going inside herself and finding the place where Marc Cage had become a part of her. She didn't know if she could. She rubbed the back of her neck and rolled her tired shoulders. She was stiff, and as weary physically as she was emotionally.

She was worried for Cage and about him. She didn't want anyone hurt. And even after what he'd done to her, after what Gavin had told her, it had become utterly important to her to have him safe.

She looked at Gavin, who was leaning forward, anxiously watching her. He was waiting for her to make the decision.

"All right," she told him. "At least I can try."

Chapter Eighteen

"I should have had a snack before leaving," Marc muttered as he drove hunched over the wheel. Even though it was night on an empty road, his eyes were burning. His skin ached as it healed from the day's sunburn; his head ached as well. And he was thirsty. He hadn't expected to be thirsty so soon.

As flippant as the words were, Marc meant them on many levels. The first few hours hadn't been so bad, except for missing Josephine so much that the ache was almost physical. He'd grown increasingly aware of her agitation, of her worry. All he wanted to do was turn around and save her, even though logic told him she wasn't in trouble. She was safe, probably just having to deal with the mess he'd left her with. But the worry was slowing his escape. He kept going, but sometimes he found himself driving at only a few miles an hour. This was not hastening his escape.

And now his pain was physical as well as in his mind, and deep in his soul. He felt like hell, and all because he was bonding. That could soon be disastrous. It was also totally unexpected.

I shouldn't have let her go.

He'd always heard that the greatest thing that could happen to a Prime was finding a bondmate. Whether the bond was with a vampire female or with a mortal was of little concern to the Prime who found this permanent sexual and soul connection. It was the highest of highs, the greatest achievement of an adult male's life. Or so young males were led to believe.

But nobody ever talked about what it was like when you were separated from that mate. You learned about the glory, but what about the hell? He wasn't even fully bonded—the connection was new, tenuous at best, yet he missed Josephine as though a part of himself had been cut out and left behind. His soul bled more with every mile that stretched between them.

But he had to let her go, to keep her safe. It was the right thing to do. He'd find her again, explain everything to her, share everything with her, and complete the bond. But only after his world was secure for the vampire Families, the

Clans, and even for the Tribes. The vampire world had to be safe before he could bring Josephine into it.

Chivalry is for idiots.

His fangs ached and throbbed, and his mouth had grown so sensitive that even sucking in a breath was agonizing. The burning was starting in his veins. It was only a faint trace of fire now, but it would grow into a maddening inferno if not dealt with soon. He needed blood.

He should have taken more than a few drops the last time they made love, but he hadn't been thirsty then. He'd only wanted to increase the pleasure for both of them. He should have drunk from Josephine before he left her, but he'd been so intent on doing the noble thing that it hadn't occurred to him.

Stupid.

Love made a male stupid. That was the only explanation for why he hadn't done something so necessary for his very survival.

If the bastards hadn't starved him, he wouldn't still be hungry. If they hadn't done things that nearly nullified the drugs that allowed him to dwell in the daylight world, he'd be able to control the blood craving better. Meditation might help if he had the time or energy for it.

Her blood would help more.

He tried not to think about what he needed and concentrated as hard as he could on driving. He was heading south toward Mexico on a rough mountain road. The track paralleled larger highways that would make the trip faster and easier. The gas tank was getting low, and, as much as he wanted to avoid people, he was going to have to turn toward a town at the next crossroads.

Or maybe not yet. The sunburn from driving in the daylight should have healed, but it was still bothering him. Even moonlight bothered him, though he was wearing sunglasses. Another day of driving in the light wasn't possible; he'd end up with third-degree burns. That agony would drive him to ground in the first dark place he came to, and he'd be helpless until he healed. They'd find him then, for sure.

He needed to find a place of his own choosing, while he was still in control, where he could hide from the blisteringly bright sunlight. Arizona was not vampire country. He didn't even understand how mortals could live in a place where the sky was cloudless, and the sun had no mercy.

Jo could explain it to him, he was sure, and with verve and enthusiasm. His Girl Scout was a native of a place called Phoenix, for the goddess's sake! She was from firebird country, and she probably loved the heat and the endless sky and the parched earth.

"We're moving to New York, hon," he told his absent lady. "As soon as I get things straightened out."

He wondered how long it would be before he could get back to her, then ruthlessly put the thought aside. The rule of survival was to concentrate only on survival. Since meeting Josephine, he kept forgetting that.

Up ahead, he spotted a crack in the cliff face. As he got closer he saw that it was actually an opening into a narrow canyon. It was wide enough to accommodate the Jeep, so he turned into it and cautiously drove a few hundred feet, carefully searching the canyon walls on either side for a place to hide from the sun. There was an overhang of rock above the point where the canyon ended, which would provide enough shelter. He'd hole up for the day. He backed the Jeep up to turn it around, then parked facing toward the road. After he draped Josephine's sleeping bag over the windshield to block out even more light, he got into the backseat, drank a couple liters of water, and tried to get into a comfortable position. It was cool and dark now, but he knew the interior of the Jeep was going to turn into an oven during the day. Still, that would be better than being exposed to the sunlight.

He'd long ago learned how to fall asleep anywhere, but when he closed his eyes he found it impossible to clear his mind. He was all too aware of his connection to Josephine. It was as if she were nearby, coming closer.

Marc told himself that was wishful thinking, and fought down his burning thirst to finally get to sleep.

"You're sure?" Gavin asked.

"Yes." Jo was growing irritated at the way he kept questioning her. They were seated together in the backseat of a Humvee. "I thought you said you believed I'm linked to Cage?"

"I do. It's just that we're on the clock here." He put his hand over hers. She didn't like him touching her.

There were two men in desert camouflage uniforms in the front seat. They wore helmets and headsets, body armor, and both were heavily armed. There was another Humvee full of soldiers in front of them, and a third behind. There were also a couple of large vans and a boxy vehicle she assumed to be an ambulance. None of the vehicles in the convoy had any official markings, and the hard-faced soldiers wore no insignia on their uniforms.

Jo had noticed these details when she was brought out of the Kennedyville police station and saw the waiting vehicles and personnel lined up along the narrow street. When she'd asked Gavin about it, his answer was to hustle her into the back of the Hummer as he said, "This is a classified operation."

Once everyone was in their vehicles, he'd asked her, "Which way?" and he'd been asking all the questions since.

Jo was getting more and more anxious as the convoy wound its way up a narrow mountain road. She knew these people were here to help Cage, but the show of force bothered her. Surely he could be persuaded to surrender without a fight. He'd seemed very dangerous when they first met, but as the days went by he'd shown kindness, and humor, and he'd seemed lucid most of the time.

She hated the thought of their hurting him, but she couldn't blame them for not taking any chances that he could hurt them.

"I don't want anyone to get hurt," she told Gavin.

"Do your job, sweetheart, and no one will."

His condescending attitude set her taut nerves even further on edge.

"Close your eyes," he said. "Think about Marc."

She pushed his hand off her arm, then she closed her eyes.

They were near, very near.

"He's hurting," she said. She felt an echo of his distress. "Hurry."

She felt the surge of power as the driver obeyed. Messages were relayed over headsets, the men speaking in military acronym shorthand that she didn't understand. With her eyes closed, she was more aware of her other senses. Sunlight came through the back window, hot on her cheek despite the air conditioner. It was a blisteringly hot day, and she could smell the smoke of the wildfires. She was grateful that Marc had gone south of the fire zone.

"He's trying to get to Mexico," she said.

"Now?" Gavin asked.

"No."

"What's he doing now?"

She felt almost hypnotized, answering Gavin's softly spoken questions while she drew abstract images and directions out of her subconscious. "Sleeping," she answered. "Dreaming."

"Dreaming of what?"

That seemed like an odd question. What difference did it make to the operation?

She answered, "Me."

Outside the cave mouth, the world was gray and cold. The only warmth came from the woman he held in his arms.

"I don't like this," she said. "It doesn't feel right."

"Tell me about it." He looked around, peering through swirling fog and seeing nothing. He sensed monsters out in the mist, invisible, waiting. They were going to have to make a run for it, they both knew it. He looked back at her. "It's you I'm worried about."

"You can't protect me from everything."

"I can try."

"Let's do this together."

He drew her closer and kissed her, gently at first. But she was life to him, she was everything to him, so soon the kiss turned ruthless and demanding. His hands moved over her in the same way. He found her breasts, squeezed them and played with her nipples, then his hands moved down her body and between her legs. His caresses were not gentle, but she groaned into his mouth, ground her body against his. She was just as needy, totally in sync with his need. Soon he backed her against the cave wall, holding her up. One hard thrust brought him inside her, where she was hot and wet and so very tight. He loved the weight of her ass in his hands, loved the way she wrapped her legs and arms around him, loved the smell of her arousal and the taste of her mouth. He pounded into her with frantic intensity. He was aware of the lurking danger beyond the cave, and the danger added desperation to their mating. This might be the last time they ever came together. The last time . . .

Then an orgasm rippled through her, and the way her sheath tightened around his cock was the trigger that set off his own explosive release. The world went blinding, white-hot.

And while he turned to ash, the danger outside drew nearer.

"They're closing in," she said.

He heard her, but he couldn't see. His eyes were open, but the fog had turned to white heat haze, with ominous shadows flitting deep inside the shimmer. He'd lost control, he'd dropped his guard. The enemy was taking advantage of his lapse, and they were going to pay.

"I'm sorry," he said. "I'm sorry."

"Just run!" she shouted. "Wake up and run!"

The warning brought him awake, but even as

he came up out of the dream, he knew it was too late.

"Cage!" he heard Josephine call, somewhere in the far, far distance. "Run!"

He felt her in pain then, sharp as a needle driven into his mind. All he could do was roar in fury, and react.

The wave of absolute, blinding pleasure drove Jo to her knees. She wasn't aware of the soldiers moving cautiously toward the Jeep, or of Gavin standing beside her. For a moment her surroundings disappeared, and she was lost with Cage in the dream, joined body and soul. Then they split apart, the world flashed into focus, and she was acutely aware of who she was, where she was, and the danger—

"Cage!" she shouted as she sprang back to her feet. "Run!"

Gavin swung around as she shouted, slapping her so hard that she fell. She landed hard on the stony ground, her ears ringing and tears of pain obscuring her vision. But when Cage's roar of outrage sounded through the midday heat, Jo was on her feet again, running toward the sound.

Glass shattered as Cage erupted out of the Jeep. He rushed out of the shadows, all muscle, speed, and fury. Orders were shouted, someone threw a metal cylinder. It landed on the ground and burst. Stinking smoke billowed into the air. Another cylinder landed, then another. Cage kept coming. Jo kept running toward him through the acrid fog. The stuff burned her nostrils and mouth with a familiar stench and taste.

Gavin ran after her, but she eluded him. She only slowed when Cage lifted his hand, pointing it toward her.

She'd forgotten about her gun until the moment before Cage fired it. Gavin tackled her, throwing them both to the ground as the bullet whipped by overhead.

A coughing fit took Cage before he could fire again. Jo managed to twist out from under Gavin and caught sight of Cage as he stumbled to his knees, caught in a cloud of smoke. He fell forward onto his hands, then reared up again, his breath coming in harsh gasps. His skin had gone white, and he seemed to be choking to death.

Their gazes met for a moment. Though his eyes were glowing like dying red coals, the look of betrayal he turned on her tore her heart in two. Then the coughing took him even harder, and the gun dropped from his hand.

That was when the soldiers who had circled him began firing. Blood stained his arms, and a red stain spread across his white T-shirt at the left shoulder. The force of the bullet impacts threw him onto his back.

"No!" Jo shouted. She turned on Gavin in anguished fury. "You weren't going to hurt him!" When she fought to get away, he shoved her hard to the ground.

He got up and walked over to where Cage lay, his face turned toward the sun, and used his foot to turn Cage onto his stomach. One of the soldiers came up and fastened handcuffs around Cage's wrists.

Jo got to her feet and stood bent over, clutching her side, and finally recognized the smell that was so thick in the smoke. It was garlic.

Garlic? That couldn't be right. How could something as harmless as garlic be so toxic to Marcus that it weakened and choked him?

She didn't know whether he was alive or dead, but she had to get to him. She'd feel it if he were dead, wouldn't she?

She moved toward the circle of men surrounding Cage, but one of the soldiers grabbed her by the arm.

"Should I put her with the others, sir?" he called to Gavin.

Others? What others?

Gavin backed away from Cage's prone form, and two men hurried forward with a stretcher.

"The woman, sir?" the soldier asked. "Should I take her to the van?"

Gavin turned her way. "No," he said to the soldier. He smiled. "I've got a better use for the bitch. Put her in with the creature. The vampire's going to be hungry when he wakes up."

Chapter Nineteen

"Please, God, don't let him be dead!"

They'd dumped the stretcher with Cage's limp body unceremoniously onto the floor, pushed her in after him, and locked them inside. The vehicle wasn't an ambulance; it was a mobile prison cell.

And it was her fault they were trapped in it. Her fault Cage was hurt—or worse.

A grid of bright lights shone down from overhead, reflecting with painful intensity off the highly polished silver walls and floor. Squinting, Jo knelt by Cage's side as the vehicle began to move slowly over the rough ground. The heat from overhead was as intense as the desert at midday.

She placed his head in her lap, then put her fingers on his neck, hoping to find a pulse. One hand hovered over his mouth, hoping to detect breathing. After a few intense minutes, she thought she felt both, but so faintly that what she sensed might only be hope and imagination. She finally decided that he was alive because she *felt* that he was.

"I'd know," she told him. She ran her hands across his heavily stubbled chin and the rough new growth of dark hair on his head. "I know."

"Hey!" she yelled. "This man needs a doctor!" She didn't think anybody heard her, but she had to try.

It was frightening that they'd gone to so much trouble to capture Cage, yet no one cared about his wounds. They wanted him alive, didn't they? Of course, Gavin had called him a vampire, and maybe vampires didn't need doctors.

Despite the hot lights, Jo shivered as she remembered what Gavin had said.

The vampire's going to be hungry when he wakes up.

Was Cage *really* a vampire?

Huge, heavily muscled Marcus Cage wasn't anybody's image of a vampire. Vampires were skinny and sepulchral-looking, like David Bowie in *The Hunger*. But—

Had the clues been staring at her all along, and she'd simply ignored them? Was she that stupid?

Gavin had certainly played her for a fool. And Cage—what had Cage played her for?

Whatever his game had been, she couldn't believe that he deserved to be Gavin's prisoner. And he would have escaped if it wasn't for her.

Jo wiped sweat off her brow with the back of her hand. Her clothes were damp and sticking to her hot skin. Why was it so bright in here?

Because vampires couldn't stand too much light?

She ran a hand along the smooth surface of the floor. It looked and felt like it was made of the finest silver; her great-grandmother's antique silver tea service had felt just like this. She tried to remember what she knew of vampire legends. Were they supposed to be allergic to silver? Silver crosses, maybe, but there weren't any crosses in sight, and . . .

"What the hell—?"

She'd noticed a slight rippling movement beneath the skin of Cage's wounded shoulder. She bent forward for a closer look, and jerked back with a gasp when the thing beneath his skin moved again. Then the bullet, flattened and covered in blood, slowly emerged from the entry wound. Rejected from Cage's body, it stuck for a moment in a bloody fold of T-shirt, then fell into Jo's outstretched hand.

She'd never been so surprised at anything in her life. It was enough to make her dizzy—or maybe that was just the heat from the lights. She held the small piece of metal up in front of her eyes. Despite the impossibility of what she'd just witnessed, she was holding the evidence in her palm. Cage's body had spat out the bullet!

She flung it away and looked at his wounds. Blood crusted his arms, but new skin had already grown over the bullet holes. And now that the bullet was out, the shoulder injury was already healing.

"Good God Almighty," she murmured. "What is going on here?"

"Blood," Cage said, as if in answer to her question. His nostrils flared, scenting the air, and he turned his head and snapped at her.

She saw the sharp fangs, and skittered backward before his teeth could close on her flesh.

She didn't recognize the monster that heaved up off his back and twisted onto his knees.

Marc could smell the scent of her blood, sense the warmth of her body, and the spike of fear that shot from her hit him like a blow. But he couldn't see her. His hands were bound in silver, there was silver all around him, and light poured into his eyes and over his skin—burning, blinding. He was helpless, hungry—and furious.

"Traitor!" he shouted at the woman he could sense but couldn't see.

"Fangs!" she shouted back, her voice shaking. "You've got fangs!"

All the better to kill you with.

"Stay out of my mind!"

He lunged toward the voice. Everywhere the silver touched hurt, reaching him through the many rips in his clothes. The bright sunlamps burned him, searing every bit of bare skin. Blood loss made him weak and even thirstier than he'd been before the ambush. And he could still feel the sharp tang of garlic gas in his nostrils and lungs. He bent over, choking and coughing in reaction to the stuff. He was almost thankful for the fit, because fighting for oxygen forced him to make a conscious effort to breathe, which forced him to think. And thinking kept him from following the instinct to fall on Josephine Elliot, rip her throat out, and drink every drop of her blood.

Oh, he'd take her blood, all right, and he'd take her. He'd make it hard and brutal, and make her love it. She deserved what she got—but he wasn't going to kill her. He fought that urge off; he was not a murderer.

He *was* a wreck. Gavin had counted on his having a multitude of bad reactions, and that planning had paid off. It took a lot to bring down a Prime, but Gavin knew the tricks to do it, which was no one's fault but his own. He'd gotten himself into this mess the day he trusted a mortal. He obviously hadn't learned his lesson the first time, since the second mortal he'd trusted had betrayed him as well.

This betrayal hurt so much that he threw back his head and howled with the pain, pain that was far worse than all the physical torture.

Jo crouched in the farthest corner of the silver box and covered her ears as Cage howled. He was an animal! How had she ever thought him to be anything else? He was the creature that ran out of the night, who assaulted her, hurt her, took her away from her life! Now look where she was—locked in a cage with him, left alone with him to be his prey.

"This is all your fault!" she shouted. It was a stupid thing to say to a monster.

"My fault?" Marc shouted back. "I'm not the one who turned me in."

Why was he bothering to argue with her? Where was he getting the strength to argue? He inched closer to her, sliding painfully across the hot metal surface.

She kicked at him. "Keep away from me."

"That's not going to happen." He ignored the

impact of her foot against his thigh. His hands were fastened behind his back. That would slow his subduing her, but it wasn't going to stop him.

"You've got an erection."

Her disgust amused him. "Comes with the territory. The fangs and the penis are connected."

"Isn't that typically male?" She kicked at him again, then lunged forward, trying to get past him.

He let her move out of the corner, then turned and followed her scent to the other side of the mobile prison cell. Marc was thrown forward when the vehicle hit a bump. He landed on top of Josephine, who'd landed on her back. Finding her and pinning her down had almost been too easy.

Her fists found his shoulders and the sides of his head as he scrunched forward. The lights kept him blind, and his hands were useless, but his weight and strength were enough to control her.

He found a soft, bare spot of skin, and bit down. She arched with pleasure as he drank from her, so he gave as well as took. The nourishment didn't stop his suffering, surrounded by light and silver, but it helped the weakness, helped hold madness at bay.

But he couldn't take everything he wanted; it

wasn't possible without the use of his hands. Yet even if he'd managed to get his cock out of his pants, he couldn't bring himself to rape her. His conscience would only let him go so far.

He ended up only taking a few sips of blood; enough to sustain him, but not enough to weaken her. *Saving a valuable resource,* he told himself. When he got a chance to run again, he was going to need his hostage healthy and strong.

"Move," Jo demanded. "Get off of me."

"No," he answered, his voice muffled against her skin.

She kept her eyes closed against the glare of the hot lights. If it was this bad for her, it must be unbearably painful for Cage. His head was buried between her breasts. She doubted they were giving him a lot of shelter, as they weren't all that big.

She wondered how far they'd gone, and where, while she'd gone in and out of a semiconscious blissful fog. At least they'd finally turned onto a relatively smooth, straight road. Her back ached, a foot was asleep, and his weight was hot and heavy on her. It was too intimate, as well as uncomfortable.

"I don't want you touching me."

"I don't want to touch the floor. All I've got to rest on is you."

"I'm not a piece of furniture."

"You'll do."

He sounded so very angry and contemptuous, and she didn't know why it bothered her.

"You *bit* me, Cage." She remembered how it felt, the sharp intrusion of fangs sinking into her arm, the swift, hot pleasure that followed. Her body was still alive with the electric aftershocks of that pleasure.

"Biting's what I do."

He sounded totally unapologetic, which infuriated her. "It's wrong. You should have asked."

His head came up. Though his eyes were screwed tightly shut, she could feel him glaring at her. "Wrong?" His deep bass voice rang like a bell in her head. "You turned me in! You got me into this—"

"*Us* into this," she corrected angrily. "You're not the only one locked in this box. With a vampire. Who bites without permission."

He really is a vampire. How stupid was she not to have figured that out on her own? And why had the revulsion already worn off? Because the actual process of his taking her blood gave her orgasms? She hadn't asked for the pleasure, and experiencing it was no reason to forgive him for doing it.

"You shouldn't take people's blood."

"How else am I supposed to live?"

"I've seen you eat food."

"It's not the same thing. Food provides some energy, but I need human nourishment to really live." He sneered, which looked oddly menacing with his eyes closed. "You're skinny and kind of anemic, but you were all I could get. Traitor," he added.

His words stung her. No, the pain went deeper than a sting. That he could hurt her by insulting her quality as a food source showed how insane this situation was.

"I'm not sane," he said, picking up her thought. "I'm barely in control. Don't push me to do what Gavin wants."

"What does Gavin want?"

"For me to kill you. That's what you deserve for what you did to me."

"I didn't do anything to you!"

"What did Gavin promise you? Though it doesn't matter, now, does it?"

"You don't have to sound so pleased about my being a prisoner, too."

"I need any pleasure I can get. After all, I'm the one they're going to dissect, slowly."

Her stomach knotted at his words. Wild dream images of torture and humiliation rose in her mind, only they hadn't been dreams at all. Cage was being taken back to the white laboratory. And so was she.

She said, "If they went to so much trouble to capture you alive—"

"If you hadn't *helped* them capture me alive, I—"

Jo didn't notice that the vehicle had stopped until the door was flung open. A blast of cool night air flooded the silver cube as armed men swarmed in, and she and Cage were grabbed and dragged outside.

Where Gavin was waiting.

Chapter Twenty

The prison vehicle and the rest of the convoy were parked inside the center of a huge square compound surrounded by high metal fences. Guard towers spiked up at intervals, and tall floodlights reflected off the razor wire circling the top of the fences. There were several long, low buildings nearby, and a concrete roadway stretched off into the dark. Not a road, Jo decided; a runway. The compound had the look of a small military base.

Gavin gave her a quick look as she stood between two armed men, then he turned his attention on Cage. A pair of men held Cage by the arms, while others surrounded him at a cautious distance of a few feet. A lot of weapons were trained on the vampire.

"Marcus, old buddy," Gavin said. "You look like shit."

Jo watched as Cage summoned up energy and bravado from somewhere to straighten his shoulders and turn a wide smile on Gavin. "I feel like it, too—buddy."

"Bet you wish I'd just kill you and get it over with."

Cage inclined his head in a gracious gesture that was elegant despite his big, burly figure. "If you wouldn't mind."

"I would for old time's sake, if it paid." Gavin shrugged, and jerked a thumb back toward Jo. "At least you got laid while you were on the loose."

Cage's expression went blank, and he pressed his full lips together.

"A gentleman never tells, huh? Never mind, she told me all the details." Cage remained silent, and Gavin motioned to the armed crowd surrounding him. "You know where to put him. And if he gets out again," he added, as they began to drag him away, "you're all dead."

Jo's heart wrenched as she watched Cage disappear. She started to step after him, but the guards caught her by the arms.

A tall, lean man with graying brown hair approached Gavin from one of the buildings. "So you finally brought the creature in."

"Told you I would," Gavin answered. "The Patron will be happy."

"The Patron will be happy when our goals are accomplished."

"You can't accomplish anything without a vampire, and I'm the one who captured him. And remember, I wasn't here when he escaped. It's your research team that let him get away."

"There is no need to assign blame," the other man said. "I merely commented that you returned our subject."

"I didn't hear you congratulating me, Brashear."

Jo struggled with her captors as the men talked. "Sir," one of the men holding her finally called. "What do we do with this one?"

Gavin and Brashear turned to look at her while she futilely fought against being held.

"What's this?" Then Brashear gestured toward a trio of scared-looking women who were being hustled out of one of the vans that had been in the convoy. "And what are they doing here?" Jo recognized the women from the restaurant.

Gavin put a hand on Brashear's narrow shoulder and gestured toward the other prisoners. "Remember how you said that one of the problems you've had with the subject might be caused by not providing him with primary source protein? Since none of us wants to provide it, I brought in some blood donors. Now he can drink it fresh out of the bottle."

"Ah," Brashear said, and nodded. "That might prove to be a good idea."

"Might?" Gavin shook his head, and laughed. "You'll thank me when old Marcus starts fattening up. Starving him didn't get you what you wanted; it just got two of your people killed."

"Not to mention the significant damage to equipment and the compromise of experimental results."

"And he escaped," Gavin added.

"Sir?" the guard questioned once again. "Should we put the woman with the other prisoners?"

"No." Gavin stepped up to her. "She's a present for you, Brashear."

"Really?" the other man asked. "What interest does she hold for my research? What am I supposed to do with her?"

"Cut her up in little pieces, for all I care." Gavin grasped Jo by the chin and jerked her head up, then he stroked two fingers along her throat. "I'm sure you'll want to take samples of the spots where Marcus has been sucking her blood."

"Useful," Brashear agreed.

"What's even more interesting is that he's been fucking her. Fucking and sucking enough for her to be in mental contact with the vampire."

"Really?" Brashear stared intently at her. Jo saw the excitement in his pale eyes and the slight flush of color in his narrow cheeks. And she recognized him as one of the torturers from the white room nightmares.

"Get away from me!" she shouted on a surge of panic. "Get him away from me!"

Gavin laughed.

"Really?" Brashear said again, ignoring her reaction. The word held a terrifying amount of glee. "Get her secured on one of the examination tables immediately."

Gavin stroked her throat again before the guards took her away. "Good-bye, sugar," he said. "It's been fun for me." He was smiling when he added, "This isn't going to be fun for you at all."

Jo hurt all over, but at least they'd given her a shower and dressed her in a clean white nightgown. The scientists were downright paranoid about not getting any dirt in their precious white torture room. Blood, yes; dirt, no.

She wrapped her arms around her drawn-up legs and rested her head on her knees. She felt like Han Solo after Darth Vader had him tortured to get Luke Skywalker's attention. "They didn't even ask me any questions," she murmured wearily.

They had examined her all over with painful, humiliating thoroughness. They'd stuck syringes in her, extracted stuff, injected stuff, attached monitors and probes. They'd even done a dental exam. A lot of what they'd done had hurt; all of it had been frightening and wearying. She was used to pain, and to medical tests and exams; but there had been nothing helpful or healing in the impersonal treatment. She was just a guinea pig to her captors. Neither her protests nor even her occasional screams had drawn any response from them.

When they were finished they'd dragged her here, where she'd slept until a nightmare woke her up. In the nightmare she searched for Cage, but couldn't find him. She woke depressed and disoriented—because he wasn't there.

She was sitting on one of the cots in a large, windowless barracks room. The walls, floor, and ceiling were painted a dull gray, with rows of industrial-style fluorescent lights overhead. A large metal door was the only access. She knew there was an armed guard stationed on the other side of it. Besides the cots, the room held a long table with benches, a toilet and sink, and two of the three women Gavin had taken from the restaurant in Kennedyville— the waitress and the cashier. She wondered where the third woman was.

Jo was glad she wasn't alone. She knew that was selfish, but couldn't help feeling that way right now. She also felt like she ought to apologize for having gotten the women into this.

Worst of all, despite everything, she missed Cage. She worried about him. She knew now that the dreams they'd shared had been memories, or premonitions. It was hard knowing how to define psychic/telepathic stuff, but the two of them were connected—for good or ill. Yet she couldn't feel him now. She felt empty, like something vital had been pulled out of her. Her soul, maybe?

She was terrified of what they must be doing to Cage to have caused this break in their connection. How were they hurting him? What experiments were they running?

He is a vampire, she reminded herself.

Vampires were evil creatures of the night, blood-drinking parasites who preyed on humans. She tried to harden her heart, but the worry kept resurfacing. Just because he was a vampire didn't mean he was a bad person. So far, Marcus Cage had behaved in a far more morally superior fashion than Gavin, his troops, or the gang of scientists. Most of the time.

But—

I miss him.

"I see you're awake," the waitress said. She came over and sat on the cot next to Jo's. As she did, the roar of a jet engine streaked by close over their heads, shaking the building.

"What was that?" the waitress asked, when the noise had faded enough to be heard.

"Gulfstream," Jo answered.

"Are we at an air force base?"

Jo shook her head. "That type of plane's used by corporations or private owners."

The other woman eyed her curiously. "How do you know that?"

"I used to be a pilot. That sounded like a Gulfstream's engines to me."

"A private plane?" The woman sounded desperate when she went on. "But we're at a military base, right? The government's holding us in a quarantine, right?"

"I don't think so," Jo answered.

"But the sheriff came in with some soldiers. They did blood tests. They told Marcia, Karen, and me that we were candidates. For what? And where's Marcia?"

Jo knew exactly why the other women had been taken prisoner, and a hard, hot fist of jealousy curled in her gut, as crazy as that was. The women were scared, and as helpless as she was. There was no reason for her to be angry with them.

"I'm Debbie," the woman told her.

"Jo Elliot," Jo introduced herself.

"I remember you coming in, and all the food you ordered before the sheriff took you away. This is Karen," Debbie said, as the cashier came to sit beside her. "Why did the sheriff take you away?" she asked.

Karen looked at Jo suspiciously. "You infected us with some disease, didn't you? That's why we're locked up here. Is this your fault?"

Jo shook her head. Though if she hadn't called her mother, her mother wouldn't have called the local sheriff's office, and the sheriff then wouldn't have contacted Gavin. Did the local police believe Gavin was a government agent? *Was* this really a secret government project? No, she couldn't believe that.

Cage had warned her that the people chasing him had an unlimited budget, and that cops could be bought. She was fairly certain that bribe money had led directly to where they were right now, and she also knew that her mom was going to have the Kennedyville sheriff's ass. That was the first comforting thought she'd had for a long time.

Just then the door opened at the other end of the room. The third woman was pushed inside, and the door slammed shut behind her. Debbie and Karen rushed to the dazed Marcia as the woman staggered forward. Jo got up and followed.

"What happened to you?" Debbie asked. The waitress took Marcia by the arm and led her to sit on one of the benches by the long table. She sat beside her and put her arm around Marcia's shoulders.

Jo held back, watching them. She guessed that they were longtime friends. She was the outsider, even more than she was used to being.

She'd lost her empathic abilities, and wasn't yet used to dealing with people on a normal basis. All she had to go on was body language, facial expressions, and tones of voice. She'd totally messed up in reading Gavin. She had to go cautiously, observe, guess.

Marcia was the youngest and best-looking of the three women, with a shapely figure and short red hair. That gave Jo a good idea about why

why Marcia'd been taken first. Debbie was somewhere in her forties, attractive in a rounded, matronly way. Karen was tall, tanned, sharp-featured, and flat-chested; somewhere in her thirties, Jo thought.

"You all right, honey?" Debbie gave Marcia an encouraging squeeze. "Tell us what happened."

Marcia's answer was a moan and to wipe tears off her cheeks.

"What's wrong?" Karen asked. The cashier knelt beside Marcia and took the woman's hands in hers. "You're cold."

"He—" Marcia began. She looked up, and met Jo's gaze. "He has red eyes."

Jo nodded slowly. "Sometimes," she said. She took a step forward. "Is he all right?"

Karen shot to her feet, rounding on Jo. "Who is he?" She turned back to Marcia. "Red eyes?"

"He wouldn't eat me," Marcia told Jo. "He said to tell you that you were on the menu, and nobody else."

"Eat?" Debbie asked. A note of panic entered her voice. "What do you mean—'eat'?"

"He doesn't *eat* people," Jo said. "He just drinks blood." She touched her throat and her wrist. "It's not bad at all, really." She didn't know why she was defending Cage, and she knew she wasn't doing a good job of explaining.

"He's crazy," Marcia said. "They put me in a cell with a crazy man. He crouched in a corner and stared at me for the longest time. Sometimes his eyes glowed. And he had long teeth—like a wolf."

"Like a vampire," Jo said. Debbie and Karen looked at her like she was crazy. "You should get used to the idea of vampires being real," she said. "It will save you a lot of trouble in the long run."

"He was hungry," Marcia said. "He yelled at me about how hungry he was. He's got a deep voice like—"

"A former Marine sergeant."

"—a wild animal."

"Oh, please! Did he hurt you?"

"He wanted to." Marcia gave Jo an angry look. "Because I wasn't you!"

Jo was taken aback. Part of her wanted to think that Cage wanted no one's blood but hers because of an emotional attachment. Then she told herself that the emotion was hatred. He wanted to drain her dry out of revenge.

She put her hand to her throat, and as she did, the door opened once more. All the women came to their feet; the trio huddled together nervously while Jo faced the intrusion alone.

A pair of guards entered. Gavin followed them. The handsome blond man turned a courtly smile on the other women. "Hope you're comfortable, ladies." Then he turned his attention to Jo. "Come along," he said. "Someone important wants to meet you."

Chapter Twenty-one

Everyone in the luxurious meeting room but Gavin looked nervous. Even blank-faced Brashear had a tense air about him. Good. If she had to be handcuffed to a chair, she was glad that she wasn't the only one who was uncomfortable. Gavin leaned against a wall, watching the door with his arms crossed.

They'd marched her across the compound in the midday heat. She had bare feet and was wearing only the short white gown that did nothing to protect her from the sun. Gavin had left the guards outside the three-story building and brought her to this room on the top floor, where Brashear and two of his people were seated at a large conference table. Gavin put her in a deep leather chair and cuffed her wrists to the armrests. No one looked at her, no one spoke; all kept their tense attention on the door. Jo looked around.

The office had a large picture window with a panoramic view of buildings, the guard towers, a hangar, and the sleek Gulfstream jet sitting on the baked concrete runway. There was another plane sitting in front of the hangar, with a pair of techs in coveralls lazily working on it. There were a lot of vehicles parked in the compound, including Hummers, Jeeps, and several three-wheeled all-terrain vehicles. Armed men wearing desert camo patrolled the fenced perimeter.

Beyond the prison was empty desert, with a jagged row of mountains in the distance. The sky was pitiless blue, the earth seared red-brown. It was not a friendly, hospitable view; but she would gladly have run out into the arid, baking desert and taken her chances rather than be locked up with these people. The compound didn't have the spanking-new look of something that had been built specifically for this operation, but the buildings looked very well maintained.

Jo suspected the facility was part of an old, abandoned military base.

"This is a privately funded evil conspiracy, isn't it?" she asked.

Gavin gave a snort of laughter, and one of the seated men looked her way. He had red hair, freckles, and thick glasses. "Oh, yes," he said.

Then he looked embarrassed at having spoken and turned his attention back toward the door.

Jo was about to ask who they were waiting for, when the door opened. First a pair of broad-shouldered bodyguard types walked in, then a woman carrying an old-fashioned black leather medical bag. Finally, an old man came tottering in. Everybody at the table stood up when he stepped slowly into the room; even Gavin came to attention. Jo wouldn't have stood, even if she wasn't chained to her seat. She didn't consider that her circumstances warranted showing respect for the authority figures, regardless of age.

And the old guy was *really* old. Montgomery Burns old. He looked like a cricket in a two-thousand-dollar suit. His form was bent and withered, and he used a cane. Only a few silver wisps of hair remained on his head, and there were age spots on top of his wrinkles. His ears were huge. One of the bodyguards helped him take a seat at the head of the table. Nobody else sat while he had a good look around.

His gaze met Jo's for a moment. There was nothing old or diminished in those eyes; they were as sharp as the edge of a blue steel sword. And hungry. He wanted to eat the world.

Now that, she thought, *is a vampire.*

"Gentlemen," he finally said. Despite the frailty of his body, there was still strength in his voice.

Everyone took their seats and turned nervous attention on the man at the head of the table. The bodyguards and the woman went to stand by Gavin.

"Hi," Jo called out from the other end of the table. "We haven't been introduced." She generally wasn't the sort to be a wise guy, but she'd gone beyond fear. What did she have to lose by standing up for herself at this point?

She wasn't surprised when she was ignored.

Brashear said, "Good afternoon, Patron."

"Good afternoon, Patron," the others parroted.

The old man gave a slight nod of acknowledgment.

Patron? Jo almost laughed at the medieval images the title conjured. She half expected Brashear to kneel and kiss the old guy's ring. Of course, if the old man was providing funding, security, and a vampire for these mad scientists' experiments, the researchers were probably willing to kiss anything the old man wanted.

"Report," the Patron ordered.

Gavin replied. "The subject has been secured. All traces of the search for the subject have been covered. New security measures are in place."

The Patron's cold gaze flicked ever so briefly to Gavin. "You are not going to bother to reassure me that no incident of this kind will happen again."

"No, Patron." He sounded perfectly confident that he had his end of the operation under control.

Jo hated to think that he was correct. She wanted to escape, and even though he was a vampire, she wanted Marc Cage to escape as well.

"Was the subject in contact with any of its kind?"

"I'm certain he wasn't. He'd rather die than lead us to any more of his species."

"Pity," the Patron said. "I had hoped the delay caused by the subject's escape would have some benefits."

"Patron?" Brashear held up his hand, like a schoolboy asking for attention.

The Patron turned a very cold look on Brashear. "You are behind schedule. Your work in finding the secrets of eternity is not coming cheaply. While your subject has all the time in the world, I do not. You are wasting my time. That displeases me."

The words were said with no inflection, yet they chilled the room. Jo flinched, even though she wasn't exactly unhappy to see the mad scientists in trouble with their boss.

Brashear had to clear his throat before he could talk. "Yes, Patron," he acknowledged. "But we believe that there will be major benefits resulting from the escape, despite the amount of time lost working with the subject. We now have new directions in which to take the research. A new research subject." He gave Gavin a look that was half-grateful, half-resentful. Then he looked at Jo. "Mr. Gavin brought us this female, as I mentioned when I contacted you to report that the subject was once more in custody. Test results on her connection with the subject show promise."

The Patron looked at her once more, and Jo felt like a bug under a microscope. "You said the subject fed off her, and that was good for us. How? You told me that prolonged feeding didn't cause physiological changes to a vampire's victims."

"No, Patron," Brashear dared to contradict. "I told you that it was impossible for direct contact with the subject to do you any good."

"He likes girls," Gavin said.

Jo was annoyed with herself for almost smiling. Nothing here was funny; these people were deadly serious.

Brashear got up and came around to stand behind her. He put his hands on her shoulders. Looking down, she noticed that there was a small coiled snake tattoo on the back of his left hand. She found it odd that the scientist had a tat, but a snake certainly suited his cold, reptilian personality.

She tilted her head back to look at him. "Get your hands off me."

Of course he ignored her. He was staring at the Patron. "Here is your immortality."

"That—" the Patron said dismissively, "is a vampire's food source."

"And sexual partner," Brashear added.

The old man's features twisted with disgust. "You know I don't want to hear about how the creatures copulate with humans."

"It's my understanding that the effect is not unpleasant for the victim," Brashear said.

"It rocks your world," Jo said, looking the Patron in the eye.

The Patron went red as a beet. On the other side of the room, Gavin chuckled softly.

"Prolonged sexual contact with a vampire creates psychological and physiological changes with certain human and vampire pairings," Brashear explained.

"That's how I found Cage," Gavin spoke up. "The woman's been with him long enough to have formed a connection. She led me to him."

"Only because you're a lying bastard," Jo said.

"Please allow me to return to my explanation." Brashear squeezed Jo's shoulders hard.

"Explain, then," the Patron said.

Brashear squeezed again, harder. "Stay quiet," he ordered softly. "You are here as an exhibit, not a participant." He turned his attention to the watching Patron. "Tests on the subject show that changes have begun to occur in him. The subject can still satisfy the craving for blood from any mortal source. However, he has become psychologically fixated on this woman. He can drink blood from anyone, but he *craves* her blood. This craving will give us the secret of immortality."

"Does he crave her like a drug? She's an addiction?" the Patron asked. "Will withholding her make him more cooperative?"

"The last thing we want to do is keep the pair separate, because a pair-bonding process has begun. When vampires form pair bonds with mortals, they develop a symbiotic union. This symbiosis results in the mortal partner's life span increasing to equal the vampire's."

Pair bonding? Jo felt overwhelmed. He was talking about her and Cage, wasn't he? And Brashear wanted to use this bonding—her—against Cage.

"You've used me to hurt him already." She shook her head. "Not again."

The Patron looked annoyed. "Why haven't you mentioned this before? I've relied on your expertise about vampires. Withholding information is unacceptable."

"I didn't withhold information. I assumed that this particular knowledge was irrelevant to our research. Vampire and mortal pair bonding cannot be forced. They are an accident of nature. I deal with science, not accidents. Normally."

Brashear squeezed Jo's shoulders again. "I don't believe in luck, either, but this time we got lucky. Or perhaps we created the necessary conditions. The subject was starved and desperate when he escaped. Somehow that led him to a woman with the qualities he needed to form the bond that is unique to each couple. It is this woman's blood that we will need, to discover how ingesting vampire blood leads to the increased life span."

The Patron sat back in his chair, some of the hungry tension going out of him. He looked almost benign when he asked, "Then why aren't you working on a serum right now, instead of displaying this prize captive to try to impress me?"

Brashear's hands moved up from her shoulders to stroke her throat. Jo shuddered at the utter creepiness of his touch. She was already stiff with terror, both wanting and dreading to hear the answer to the Patron's question.

"We can't do anything with her yet," Brashear said.

The Patron frowned, and the room filled with tension once more. "And why is that?"

"Because her body is still free of any contaminants."

"What?" the Patron asked. "What are you talking about? Is the woman going to be a vampire or not?"

"Of course she isn't going to become a vampire. I have told you before that a mortal cannot be changed into a vampire."

"Well, that's good to know," Jo murmured.

"The vampire must share his blood with a bondmate in order to—"

"She hasn't bitten Marcus yet," Gavin summed up. "She hasn't drunk any of his blood."

The Patron's gaze swung to Gavin. "Why not?" he demanded.

Gavin shrugged. "The mood hasn't been right for him to offer her a taste of immortal wine, would be my guess. Old Marc probably needs moonlight, candles, champagne, Sinatra. Maybe even an engagement ring before he lets a girl bite him. He's an old-fashioned kind of guy."

"Well, I'm not giving him a diamond," Jo said flippantly, trying to hide her surprise.

Brashear's hands tightened slightly around her throat. She knew she was too valuable for him to kill, but she didn't fancy being choked until she passed out, either.

"It is likely that the subject was attempting to avoid the very situation we want to create," Brashear said. "We know that he is determined to thwart our experiments, and protect his species' monopoly on longevity at any cost."

"Maybe he doesn't like me," Jo said. "I'm just a food source to him. We haven't got any sort of bond."

"But you will have," Brashear said. "Once you are introduced into the subject's environment, it will only be a matter of time before the sexual, physiological, and psychological attraction will create the necessary trigger to—"

"We don't have time!" the Patron cut him off.

"And you don't know Marcus," Gavin added. "You can treat him like an animal for any regular experiment, but you can't treat him like an animal when it involves the most important thing in his life. You've got to work him into the right frame of mind if you want him to take a mate."

Jo loathed that everyone's attention was firmly on Gavin. She'd been manipulated by Gavin into giving up Cage. She didn't like to think that she was stupid, naïve, or weak-willed. Maybe one or another, but not all of those things at once. She'd been wary of him at first, but Gavin had gotten to her, led her into doing exactly what he wanted. Could he do the same to Marcus Cage? When Cage was weak, drugged, and driven by compulsions that were part of his nature?

She was terrified of the answer.

"Tell us what you would have us do, Mr. Gavin," the Patron said.

Terrified or not, it looked like she was going to find out.

Chapter Twenty-two

$\mathcal{M}$arc paced, alone in the small cell. Alone but for the round black eyes of the monitor cameras in the ceiling that watched his every movement. He hated that they could see him, but that he was blind to his enemies' movements.

He was also blind to their thoughts. They had drugs to ensure that. The effect of the injections didn't last long, and he could feel how they had to keep upping the dosage, but the temporary mental deafness was isolating. It wasn't as if he could ever read minds at any great distance; he'd always had to concentrate hard to read minds. But he could influence thought. That was what they were really afraid of, and they believed it was the only thing he could do. They thought he was a hypnotist, not a telepath, but they were scared enough of that.

Reading thoughts was very hard if someone

had a strong will, or was at a distance, especially if you didn't have an emotional connection to the mind you were trying to contact. You had to be able to sneak up on an unsuspecting mind if you wanted to influence a person. No chance that anyone here was unsuspecting.

Of course, there was a more intimate way to share thoughts and emotions. He'd had that kind of communication with Josephine from the moment he sensed her presence in the desert. He'd cherished it, and now he hated it. Just as he hated the drugs that closed his mind, even while welcoming the release from his connection to the woman who'd betrayed him.

How could she do that? He'd let her go, and she'd made him a prisoner.

He was so thirsty for her, he wanted to scream. But he wouldn't do that, not when his enemies could hear. Not when she'd been used against him once already.

If he'd been smart, he would have taken the other woman. He used to be smart. He used to know how to take care of himself. Josephine had made him into a weak fool.

How long had he been pacing? And when would they come for him again? When they came, they came in smoke.

Marc dropped onto the edge of the narrow cot.

He'd been thinking in his own language, and forced himself to translate the concepts into modern English. To say his enemies came in smoke was all very colorful, and even true, but technically, they knocked him out with some anesthetic gas before carting him off for experiments. His people's language was evocative and romantic, but it wasn't scientifically precise.

And he couldn't think it, let alone speak it around these people. He dared not give away even linguistic clues to the origins of his kind, or how they thought. He had to think like mortals, talk like them, be like them.

Normally it wasn't hard. English was his language of choice, America the place he'd been born and raised, and served. The place where he paid taxes, had a home, where his family lived. But his Family was vampire, and he was Prime. Primes protected their own.

Even mates who betrayed them?

He nodded sharply. He couldn't help it. Her blood was in him, sustained him, called to him. Josephine was his. No Tribe sex slave could have it worse than she would, once he got his hands on her again, but she was still his. What did the Tribes call the humans they kept? Cattle? Pets?

They never trusted humans, never gave them the chance to take advantage.

Marc looked at the gray walls of his prison and deliberately let himself be aware of the pain that surged through his body. Humans—mortals— had done this to him. With the help of the one mortal he'd totally trusted.

Maybe the Tribes have the right idea.

Even as he had the thought, he became aware of the haze wavering in the air. The cell was being flooded with gas. He surged to his feet, only to fall back onto the cot, his senses reeling.

They were coming for him.

"You awake, City Mouse?"

Her hand touched his cheek softly, tenderly. Desire burned through him.

Marc grabbed Josephine by the wrist and squeezed until the pressure forced a moan of pain from her. "Don't touch me," he ordered. Then he let her go.

The mattress shifted as she got up. With the movement, Marc realized that he was lying on a bed. For a moment, he insanely hoped that he'd only dreamed of being recaptured. But he knew it was all too real when he sat up and opened his eyes.

He was still in a cell, though this one was fitted with a solid door instead of bars. As he got up and turned slowly around, he saw that this was a larger room, with more furnishings. He'd been lying on a double bed covered in fresh linens, instead of a narrow, bare cot. The concrete walls and floor were painted a golden beige instead of antiseptic white. The lighting overhead was recessed and gave off a gentle glow rather than a harsh glare. He spotted a toilet and a shower stall through a doorway, giving at least an illusion of privacy. There was also a kitchen and dining area—a table, chairs, refrigerator, and a microwave on top of a cabinet. It looked more like a studio apartment than a prison.

And there was Josephine. She'd retreated to an empty corner, where she stared at him apprehensivly, one hand over the wrist he'd bruised.

She was also naked. They both were. He couldn't help but look at her, and his body couldn't help but respond to what he saw.

It took all his willpower to turn his back on her, trying to combat the lust and thirst that were one and the same. His voice was raw with need when he croaked, "What are we doing here?"

"The luxury suite was Gavin's idea," she answered, followed by a deep sigh. "It's supposed to set a romantic tone."

"You're a naked woman," he said. "That's all

the romance I require. It's easier to bite a naked woman," he added.

"Saves you the risk of getting cloth caught in your fangs, I suppose." She sounded calm, but he could feel her fear.

"It's easier to do a lot of things with a naked woman," he added, just to see if it would spike her emotions higher.

It did; and her voice betrayed her nerves when she said, "They want you to bite me."

"Then I won't." It was a hard promise to make, especially when he was furious enough to drain the life out of her.

"They don't think you'll have a choice. Eventually, you'll be too thirsty not to. We both know what happened the night you attacked me."

She was right. The thirst was a living creature of fire inside him. It needed what it needed, despite his fight to control it. He should have taken the other woman. It would have helped bank the fire to a manageable level a while longer.

"If *they* think you're the only woman I'll touch, they're wrong."

"Then you shouldn't have told Marcia that. The red-haired woman you wouldn't touch," she added before he could ask.

"I didn't mean it."

"They don't believe that. Besides, it's not so much that they want you to bite me. They want *me* to bite *you*. They think I'm going to drink your blood. But the last thing in the world I want to do is drink anyone's blood—*especially* yours."

How could he be hurt by this rejection after what she'd already done to him?

He whirled to face her. "Will you stop talking about what *they* want? If it weren't for you, we wouldn't even have to deal with them."

Josephine came out of the corner and was halfway across the cell when she stopped to glare at him. "Me? What do you mean, *me?*"

"What did Gavin promise you? Lots of money?"

"I've got enough money," she answered. "What do I need with more?" She laughed bitterly, and touched one of her many scars. "I've got my health."

The bitter irony only stung him more. "Did he promise you immortality? To heal those scars?" He knew every word was a psychic stab wound, and he was pleased to see her pale and trembling. "You made a mistake. Because, darling, you can't get immortality from him."

"I know that," she said, blinking back tears. She made a sharp gesture. "And he didn't offer."

"Then what did he say he'd give you for turning me in?"

Josephine pressed her lips tightly together, then turned her back on him. He heard her breath catch and a stifled sob. Pain radiated from her like heat haze.

He couldn't keep away from her anymore. He stepped up behind her and put his hands on her bare shoulders before he knew he was going to do it.

She tried to shrug out of his grasp. "Don't touch me!"

"That's what you're here for."

He pulled her tightly against him. His hands moved of their own accord, down her arms and around her to caress her belly, and up her waist to cup her breasts, bringing a gasp from her when the pads of his thumbs pressed against her nipples. He almost forgot his anger with the pleasure of touching her. He breathed in her scent. He wanted her.

"What did Gavin offer you?" he asked again.

She went even stiffer. She tried to calm her emotions, tried to not even think, to hide from him. It was infuriating.

"Tell me." The words were soft, and full of menace.

"You're being a pig."

He turned her around and lifted her chin to make her look at him. "Tell me."

"You." She spat the word out like a curse. "He offered me you."

He dropped his hand and stepped back. "What are you talking about?"

"He said your life was in danger."

"Yeah. From him."

"I didn't know that!"

"You knew I was being hunted. You promised not to turn me in."

"Yes." She ran her hands up and down her bare arms; she looked cold. "But he said you were sick."

Marc grabbed a sheet off the bed and tossed it to her. As she wrapped the material around her, he sighed and rubbed his hands over his face. His head was whirling with confusion. "What did Gavin tell you about me?"

"That you were sick," she repeated.

"And?"

She looked at the floor, the ceiling, and finally back at him. "It made sense at the time."

"What did?"

"That you were an escaped convict who had volunteered for an experiment that went wrong. He said they needed to find you—so they could fix you. He said he wanted to help you."

"And you *believed* him?"

Cage's deep shout filled the room.

Jo took a step closer to confront him. "It made

a lot more sense that you merely *thought* you were a vampire, than your actually *being* one. If you had just once said you were a vampire, I might not have believed him."

"*Said?*" Marc shook his head. "Woman, I drank your blood!"

"That could have been a kinky fetish. It's not like you ever showed me your fangs while you dragged me all over the state. Maybe if you'd explained more about this—"

"Every word I told you about this place was the truth."

"But it didn't sound like the truth. It sounded like paranoid delusion. Then Gavin said it was paranoid delusion, too."

"And you believed him?"

She nodded. "Eventually. It took some convincing, but yeah."

"And you led him right to me."

"Yes, and I apologize for that. By the time I figured out that you were right, and he was wrong, it was too late. Besides, then you tried to shoot me."

"I was trying to shoot Gavin. I was so furious, all I saw was him; I didn't see that you were in the way. Now I have to be grateful to Gavin for saving you." He hurried on, not wanting to think about how he had almost accidentally shot her.

He felt some of Jo's annoyance fade. "When did you figure out I was right?" he asked.

"I don't know. I just did."

"You should have figured out Gavin was lying from the beginning. Woman, you're the most sensitive empath I've ever encountered."

"Not anymore. I can't feel anyone but you now. I'm blind and deaf." She pointed a finger at him. "You did that to me."

Marc took an annoyed step forward. "You were hurting," he reminded her. "You had a hole in your shielding a mile wide. I fixed it. I fixed you."

"You turned me off," she accused. "You tuned me to you and no one else. How is that a fix?" She turned away from him.

"I don't take without giving. I gave you shielding again in exchange for your help."

"In exchange for damn near drinking me dry, you mean."

"You could have used a transfusion," he admitted. "But I would have been dead if I hadn't done what I did."

She glared. "Well, your trade didn't work for me." She tapped a finger against her forehead. "I'm not an empath anymore."

"I didn't know."

"Neither did I, until you let me go. And then

Gavin had a sheriff pick me up. He interrogated me at the sheriff's office. It was all very official."

"He worked you," Marc said. "He's got a gift for interrogation. I've never known him to need to use force on any of his subjects. He just talks, and smiles, and makes you want to tell him everything." Somewhere in the last few minutes his anger had faded, but it flared up again at realizing that she'd been used. "But you still shouldn't have betrayed me."

She had no time for his petulance. "Get over it."

Marc hesitated for a moment. He ran a hand across the top of his head, where the dark curls were growing back. He made himself look at this tired, defiant, somewhat embarrassed woman.

Yeah, Gavin had done a number on her, and she wasn't happy with herself about it.

They were trapped.

"So what are we going to do now, Girl Scout?"

She gestured toward the kitchen area. "You want a cup of coffee?"

Chapter Twenty-three

"Better not," he answered. "I'm already a little wired." He followed her toward the kitchenette anyway. He took a seat at the small table and watched as she explored the cabinet and refrigerator. She found some plastic dishes and cutlery, and a jar of instant coffee.

"Starbuck's, this is not," she complained. "Water. Where would I find wa—"

"Bathroom," he suggested.

"Right." She came back with a cupful of water and put it in the microwave to warm.

He sniffed when she brought her cup of instant coffee to the table. "I've been away from civilization too long. That actually smells good. How do we rate all this luxury?"

"It's a ploy to get us to fuck like bunnies," she answered.

"Josephine." He shook a finger disapprovingly at her.

"Well, it is." She took a sip of coffee. Then she glanced over her cup at his naked genitalia. "And you want to."

"I always want to." He shifted in the plastic chair. He tried not to think about sex, about the thirst. Just being with her seemed to ease the painful need a little. All the anger he'd burned off in the last few minutes had helped, as well. "Go on."

"For the moment, they've decided to treat us like people instead of lab rats," she told him. "There was a staff meeting where Gavin convinced the Patron that we're more likely to form the kind of pair bond they want if we're left alone. So, no monitors, no cameras spying on us, and some basic amenities like food and a real bed." She sneered as she glanced at the double bed. "Isn't it romantic?"

"If you want romance, I'll take you to Venice."

No monitors? No cameras? He doubted their captors would risk not watching him at all times. But she'd had enough privacy and control taken away from her; it was better for her if she believed they were alone.

She put the empty cup on the table. "I'd like to

go to Venice." She gestured around their quarters. "Gavin said you were old-fashioned. A romantic."

"He'd know."

She eyed him suspiciously. "You and Gavin go back a ways, do you?"

"Yeah, we've known each other for years. We used to work together."

"In the Marines?"

"After. Long after." He glanced away, almost embarrassed to explain. "I've done some covert work for the government. Black-ops stuff. I'm the one who recruited Gavin into the agency. We worked together."

"And one day you casually mentioned that you're a vampire to him?"

"No."

"And how could you *work* for the government?"

Marc sat up straight and gave her an offended look. "Are you questioning my honesty?"

"If you really work for the government, sure."

He laughed. "Worked. Past tense. I've been out of the game for a long time."

"But how can vampires—pass as humans?"

He held out his arms, showing off his big, toned body. He had a lot of skin, and it wasn't exactly moonlight pale. "Do I look like a vampire?"

She gave him a long, thorough look, and her lips quirked in a slightly lascivious smile. Her eyes lit with warm pleasure. It was almost enough to make him blush. It was certainly enough to send lust racing through him.

"The way you look was one of the things that convinced me that you're *not* a vampire. Lestat, you ain't."

"You obviously haven't read the book. He's described as being big and broad. But that's not the point. The point is that real vampires—some real vampires—take medicines that let us live like mortals. We can go out in the daylight, tolerate garlic, and tone the silver allergy down to a rash.

"Gavin's one reason we're stuck in here. Another is that at least one of the mortal scientists who work on developing drugs for the Clans has gone renegade. You have no idea how dangerous that is," he added. "Have you met Brashear?" She nodded. "Did you notice a snake tattoo on his left hand?" Another nod. "That means he was born into the Snake Clan."

The Clans were into symbols and signs and ceremony. The Families considered most of that ancient ritual nonsense, but the Clan marks did help them identify their own.

"He's not a vampire, but he's related to one," Marcus explained.

"Related?"

"We can have children with mortals. Those children are mortal but the Family—or Clan, in his case—still owes them protection and a place in life. Brashear obviously went to work in his Clan's pharmaceutical company, developing the drugs that keep us functioning in the light. And he obviously sold out those he took a vow to protect, to come to work for the Patron. What the Patron's paying him can't be worth it—he has to know that."

"What do you mean?"

Marcus gave Josephine a sober look. "We take oaths very seriously. To break a vow to our kind is a death sentence. Brashear must hate his Clan for some reason, to do what he's doing. Or he's too arrogant to think he'll get caught."

"My impression of him is that he's not going to let anything get in the way of finding the secret of immortality. Maybe he's angry that he was born mortal," she suggested.

Marc thought about it. "Maybe he wanted to be a Prime when he grew up. Sometimes it does happen, but it obviously didn't happen to him."

Josephine surprised him when she said, "Good."

"I don't know how the Patron found Brashear, but Gavin's been a mercenary since he was kicked out of the agency." Marc gave a humorless laugh. "The normal way for a traitor to leave the agency is in a body bag, but Gavin got out before he was caught. I should have caught him," he added bitterly.

"Instead, he caught you."

"Yeah." The word came out as a low, fierce rumble.

"How did he catch you?"

Josephine leaned forward across the small table and the sheet she'd wound around her body shifted, giving him an excellent view of her nicely shaped breasts. He could just make out the tops of her nipples. It was more tantalizing seeing her this way than when she was completely naked. What was half-hidden was always more intriguing, and it would be so easy to grab the sheet and drag her onto the table and peel the material out of his way. He licked his lips as his fangs and his cock throbbed with anticipation.

Not yet. Not until she was ready. Not until she was comfortable.

Right—maybe when hell froze over. He couldn't wait that long. Marc bit down hard on his lust. He would wait as long as he could.

"How did he know you're a vampire?" she asked. "Do you take these vampire drugs? How does anyone know about vampires? Rather, how come no one knows about vampires?"

She was too interested to be afraid—of him, or where they were, and what might happen to them. Marc's head spun with hunger and desire, but he couldn't bear to disturb this moment in which she was free to be herself.

Answering her rapid-fire questions would be a an exercise in control, and it was good to have someone to share his secrets with.

And if Brashear's boys were listening? He wouldn't divulge anything that the Snake Clan traitor didn't already know. It wasn't as if he was going to reveal locations of strongholds and citadels, or any other information a mortal child of a vampire would never be privy to.

He ran his hand across his scalp again, then rubbed his jaw. He needed a shave. "Where to start? Yes, I take the daylight drugs. Every Prime has a serum formula that's unique to him. Life's more convenient using the drugs."

"Is it a cure?"

He laughed. "Why would I want to be cured of what I was born to be?"

"Yeah, I can see that. It's an ethnicity."

It soothed him that she seemed to have gotten over being appalled at the idea that there were vampires, and that he was one. As long as he wasn't biting her, that is. And as long as he wasn't offering her his blood.

He needed that completion, though; their captors were right about that. He craved the sharing as much as he needed the tasting.

He dragged his mind back to the conversation. "The drugs don't change us into *Homo sapiens;* it's more that they mimic human traits. I don't know how—I take 'em, I don't make 'em. What I know is that on a normal day I like garlic, and a walk in the sunshine isn't a way to commit suicide."

"You were sunburned out in the desert."

"I was fried. That's because some of the drugs they've used on me have made my normal reactions erratic."

Fortunately, the blood, as well as the physical and psychic presence of a bondmate, helped bring a natural balance to a Prime's world.

There was more to being a vampire than biochemistry and mutant DNA. There was a psychic component to being a vampire that was as strong, or stronger, than the physical aspects of what made them different from their mortal cousins.

Even if Brashear had been raised in the heart of the Snake Clan, there were many secrets that he wouldn't be privy to. So much information about what vampires were, what they could do, and what they needed was passed mind to mind to the young from the matriarch Matri and honored Elders. Vampire young took a long time to grow up, and most of what they were taught wasn't learned in a classroom.

Marc made himself get back to her questions. "How did Gavin find out I'm what I am? I was badly injured on a mission. A bomb went off that should have killed me. Gavin got me to a safe house and stayed with me while he waited for me to die. He was shocked when my body repaired itself. I hypnotized him, told him to forget what he'd seen."

"I bet Gavin's not the hypnotizable type. It doesn't work on everybody, you know."

He nodded. "I do now. The best I can figure is that Gavin's a low-level psychic, besides being smart and strong-willed. What I did to him wore off. When he remembered, I think he watched for other clues. We were partners for a long time, and I trusted him, got sloppy.

"Then he sold out an operation for a lot of money and disappeared. I tried tracing him for a while, with no luck. When I got tired of the game, I retired and started my own business."

She looked over his muscular form. "Bouncer?"

He folded his arms across his massive chest. "Executive chef of my own restaurant."

She looked outraged. "You're a chef?"

"I have a cookbook coming out soon. And I'm opening a new place in a Las Vegas hotel. I've been a soldier and a spy, Josephine, and probably will be again. Or maybe I'll become an archaeologist, or film documentaries. I have a long life, and I plan to do everything that interests me during it. Right now, the restaurant business interests me." He smiled at her. "I thought women like domesticated men."

She looked him over again. "You will never be domesticated."

"The saying among my people is *I am Prime*— that means I'm a big bag of testosterone that likes to hunt things. We're supposed to channel all that aggression into sex and community service."

"What kind of community service are we talking about? Running blood banks?"

He grinned. "More like saving the world from nuclear meltdowns, that kind of thing. Well, the Clans mostly do the taking-care-of-humans jobs, but some of us Family boys do the occasional Hoo-Rah thing, as well."

Her brows furrowed. "Huh?"

"Never mind. Getting back to Gavin, I assume

he sold his knowledge about me to the Patron. Brashear couldn't have worked on a Prime of the Snake Clan—"

"Why not?"

"Psychological thing," was the explanation he gave. "It's easier for a vampire to hypnotize a relative. Brashear needed to be secure about being in control. To make long story a little less long—Gavin found me, drugged me, and I ended up here. As to why no one knows about vampires . . . our legends say that thousands of years ago, vampires and humans lived together. Times changed, and we went underground. We actually live among humans, we've just learned how to protect ourselves. But enough conversation," he said, and got to his feet. "I can't take this anymore."

The thirst clawed at him, on every level. If he didn't give in to the hunger while he could still guide it, the consequences would be worse for both of them later.

He held his hand out to Josephine. "Come."

She shot to her feet, and the sheet fell down to her waist. She didn't bother to try to snatch it up to cover herself. She blinked nervously at him, though. Anticipation hummed in her, and so did dread. "What do you want?" she asked.

"I'm taking you to bed."

She stumbled backward, but he caught her before the tangled sheet caused her to fall. He lifted her in his arms, and enjoyed her surprise when her arms came around his neck. It wasn't that she didn't want him—it was just that she didn't know what to make of him. The situation didn't help her mood.

Pretend we aren't prisoners, he whispered in her mind. He carried her to the bed and gently put her down. "I have to do this," he told her as he came down beside her.

A bolt of fear flashed through her. "You have to do what?"

She tried to sit up, but Marc put his hands on her. He kissed her, first her mouth, then each lovely little breast. Then he looked her in the eyes, and said, "I have to thoroughly apologize for acting like a pig." He ran his hands over her breasts. "And you're going to lie back and enjoy the apology."

"Oh." She sighed, and arched into his touch. "Okay."

Chapter Twenty-four

"What are you doing?" Not that she didn't already know. It was just that this had been going on and on and on. He'd been covering her with sharp little nips, each one sending a wave of ecstasy through her. She was quivering like Jell-O, and starting to go crazy.

He looked up from nuzzling the inside of her left thigh. She caught a glimpse of the long, sharp fangs that he'd been stroking against her sensitized skin a moment before. There was a single drop of blood on his lower lip. He slowly licked it off. "This is what I call a tasting menu," he answered, then went back to what he was doing. Slowly.

Jo lay on the bed, her fists full of bunched-up sheets, and shuddered through several more orgasms. She looked up at the ceiling, but what Cage was doing to her sent her far away. He'd lit her on fire, and she loved the burning. When a thought did flit briefly though her head, it was that maybe he should act like a pig more often, because the apology was—

"Don't stop!" she pleaded as he came up onto his knees. Then she saw the huge erection standing up out of the dark curls at his groin and decided that maybe a little apologizing of her own was in order.

"Come here," he said, and held his hands out to her. She reached out and let him pull her up to kneel on the bed as well. She ran her hands over him. Aware of him as never before, she studied him with all her senses. He was hard all over and quivered at her touch.

When she looked at his face, she saw that he was not human. There was a deep, molten-steel glow in his half-closed eyes, and long fangs pressed against his full lower lip. These changes should have frightened her but were fascinating, instead. More than fascinating—the sight sent renewed shivers of desire through her. That a hint of fear mingled with her primal urge to mate only made the desire stronger.

"May I?" she asked, and brought an index finger up to touch a sharply gleaming tooth. He moaned, and arched away from her. For a moment, she thought he was in pain.

"Oh," she said, realizing what the matter was, and she reached down, cupping her hand around his hard, swollen cock. This time he gasped, and she began to stroke him. "Will this make it better?"

"Woman!" He threw back his head and howled. "Yes!"

She loved the feeling of control, of power. She loved Cage's big, sculpted body, the wild energy and force he was keeping in check, holding back. For her sake.

She moved forward, bringing his penis to the entrance of her vagina. She felt him there and ached to thrust her hips down, to bring him all the way deep inside her.

He held her by the waist, his body as still as he could make it, waiting for her.

She pressed close to him, electric heat going through her nipples as they brushed his chest. "It's all right," she whispered in his ear. "I'm all right. Make love to me."

The next thing she knew, he'd flipped her back onto the bed and was on top of her. He was inside her in that one hard thrust she'd longed for. She lost herself in the pounding rhythm, the earthy scents of sex and sweat, the satiny rasp of skin against skin, the shifting weight and pressure of straining bodies, and the way the barriers of me and you, him and her disappeared as their minds blended with their bodies. His pleasure built, raw and primal, and became hers. It sent her flying. As the burst of pleasure seared her his fangs pierced her flesh, drawing the bliss out for what seemed like forever.

Eventually she fell from the molten sky. She was sated, her body boneless and humming at the same time. She couldn't open her eyes, didn't even want to. She couldn't move and didn't want to do that, either. She vaguely felt his arms come around her, holding her tight and safe. It was nice. She sighed, murmured something, and rested her head against his shoulder.

She didn't know how long she slept, but she woke up smiling. It wasn't that having great sex made her forget any of the bad stuff that was happening. She and Marc Cage were prisoners in a desperate situation, but the fear and dread weren't ruling her.

She even remembered what she'd said to Cage before she fell asleep. It was a foolish thing to say under the circumstances. But it was the truth—so what the hell? And if he hadn't heard, or didn't remember, that was all right.

She remembered how terrifying it had been the first few times she'd been this close to Cage. She'd come to what she felt now despite how they'd started, not because of it. To think that

Gavin almost convinced her that Cage had brain-washed her into the feelings she had for him. Desperation had brought them together, and now she couldn't imagine a life without him.

Not that she was exactly planning a cozy little future, settled down with her personal blood-sucking fiend—though if she had to give up sex like this, she wasn't sure she'd survive.

What on earth had she done before Cage? Well, she'd masturbated occasionally because she hadn't been involved with anyone for a couple of years.

Good, he thought, overhearing her thought.

You're thinking in your sleep, aren't you? She thought back at him.

His big hand reached out and stroked her breasts, then moved down to coax open her thighs. He found the swelling bud and began playing with it. *Doing this in my sleep, too.*

She wriggled against his hand, and didn't complain as he teased her to a quick orgasm.

Consider me your own personal vibrator from now on.

Jo smiled. *No problem.*

Go back to sleep.

Don't think I can. And if you hypnotize me and make me, I won't let you play with me anymore.

Ha. You'd beg me for it. The pad of his thumb pressed down on her clit, and she sucked in a sharp breath. *Wouldn't you?*

Probably, she conceded. "Rest," she told him aloud, drawing away from him. "I really do have to get up." He opened one eye to look at her, and the worry there was enough to send an ache through her, along with anger at what he'd been through. She stroked his cheek. "I'm not leaving," she told him. *Even if the door was unlocked, I wouldn't be leaving.*

He sighed, closed his eye, and loosened his hold on her so that she could get out of bed. He drew her back into his arms as soon as she came back from the bathroom. His need to touch her was palpable, surrounding her, covering her, coveting her on a mental as well as a physical level. It was possessive, protective, comforting. It was a good feeling. There had been aspects of this from him all along, but they had been covered over by desperation and pain.

He was healing, she realized. The growing connection between them was bringing him back to the person he really was when he wasn't being tortured and starved, and the energy he was giving off was—nice.

You know, for a vampire.

His mental chuckle drifted into her head.

She also knew that he wanted the same kind of complicated possessiveness from her. He was her personal vampire. He needed her to be his personal—what?

Wife, was the answer that came from him. *Bondmate. Soul mate. Symbiote.*

Jo held on tight to his big, warm body, and thought for a while. She felt him withdraw to let her be alone with the things she needed to consider, and knew he would not intrude again until she wanted him to. This was so reassuring that she relaxed to the point of falling asleep.

She ended up dreaming about a wedding where the groom's side were pale, fanged creatures all dressed in black and the bride's side all wore crosses and brandished wooden stakes. Giles from *Buffy the Vampire Slayer* officiated. Far from being afraid, Jo woke up smiling.

This is a hell of a way to meet the man of my dreams.

Am I the man of your dreams?

No, that would be Viggo Mortensen. Or Hugh Jackman. I should have said this is a hell of a way to meet the man I want to be with.

Why not say—the man you love?

She paused. *Because it's a scary thing to say.*

You said it once.

It's a scary thing to say—under the circumstances.

Which circumstance? That I'm the vampire who got you into this mess? Or the mess itself?

I can't blame you for the mess.

I can blame me for getting you into it.

Except that I'm the one who got you recaptured.

I thought we'd worked that out.

We have. She hesitated for a bit, then added, *Except for the your-trying-to-shoot-me part.* She hadn't realized how much it still bothered her until the thought was already shared. *Was it really Gavin you were aiming at? I hate to say that he saved me—but he did.*

This hurt, and Marc cursed Gavin once more. *He made you think he was saving you. Gavin knew who I was aiming at. But, for once, I'm glad that prize manipulator did what he did. I would have hated myself for it if anything had happened to you.*

He felt her sense of betrayal slowly ebbing, and waited for her to make up her mind whether to believe him.

Maybe you shouldn't have shot at anyone, she finally thought.

I was having a bad day.

And they were shooting at you, she agreed. *But—*

I'm sorry.

Aloud, he said, "I don't want anything to come between us." He was looking at the ceiling rather than at her, but his other senses were carefully gauging her reactions.

"I can understand your being a bit ticked off at me," she said. "You thought I'd betrayed you."

"I was crazy—from the sun, the attack."

"You were pissed off."

"Very." *But I still loved you. I didn't try to hurt you.* He rolled onto his side and gently stroked her face. "No matter what I do," he whispered. "Know that I love you."

She buried her head against his chest. "Fine," she whispered against his skin. "Love me. Just don't shoot at anybody when I'm in the way, okay?"

He stroked his hands down her back. "Okay," he promised. "Will you forgive me for endangering you? Forgive me for all the times I've endangered you?" *Trust me. Please. Trust me as you would yourself.* "Can't you feel how much closer we become with every moment we're together?"

She lifted her head. "You're all I can feel." *I trust what I feel.*

But you're wondering if being empathically

aware of only me is influencing what you feel about me.

No, I wasn't wondering that. But now that you mention it . . .

I'm sorry I went too far trying to fix you. Let me make it better.

How?

We're telepathically connected right now. I just need to go deeper than this, that's all.

Will it hurt?

You won't feel a thing.

He drew her to him and began to kiss and caress her. Desire began to immediately flash through her.

"I'm—not not feeling a thing," she told him between deep, passionate kisses. She liked what she was feeling, but she was confused. "Shouldn't you be—?"

I can make love to you while I'm fixing your head. Please trust me. Surrender your mind and your body—and trust me. Let go, Josephine Elliot.

She couldn't bear breaking off the way he was making her feel. It was as if something inside her soul was opening up, layer by layer. She was blooming.

You complete me, she told him.

I know. As you complete me. You're mine.

Chapter Twenty-five

"*H*ow do you feel now?" Marc asked.

"Boneless, bruised, blissful." She stretched out on the wrecked bed linen and wiggled her fingers and toes. It had been many hours since they'd done anything but have sex. "I'm starving. And I could really use a shower."

I meant how does your emotional shielding feel? Is your empathy working right again?

"Oh. That." She was silent for a long time, lying still with her eyes closed. He lay on his side, his head propped up on his hand, and watched her. He'd never get enough of watching her.

He was aware of her senses reaching out, testing. Josephine worked on instinct rather than any training of her psychic gift, but she knew what she was doing.

You feel normal, don't you? he asked.

In balance, she answered. *More like my old self. Only—more.*

We're bonding, Marc told her. *It's nothing to be afraid of.*

Except for that doing-what-the-bad-guys-want-us-to-do part.

What they want doesn't matter. We've been bonding since the night we met.

You're pleased about that. About being with me.

I can't imagine being with anyone else. He walked his fingers over her slender form. *Have to fatten you up a bit, though.*

Because I taste good?

You taste good all over. You're delicious— mind, body, and soul.

I—Thank you, Marcus Cage. How do you feel? she added.

Marc wondered if he looked as smug as he felt. *He* felt wonderful. If they were being monitored, it would not be wise to show his improved condition. Then again, perhaps they didn't fully understand what happened when a bond formed.

They wanted him to take her blood, and he was doing just that. Drinking anyone's blood was sustaining. Blood with sex was physically and mentally satisfying. Forming a bond, sharing body and soul—that was beyond energizing. A bonded Prime was a force of nature, something to be reckoned with.

But their captors didn't understand that it wasn't all enzymes and biochemistry that made a bond. There was something magical at work, as well. Something that couldn't be duplicated in a lab, and it made all the difference in the world.

Brashear would be aware that the more Marc had of Josephine's blood, the more he would want to give his blood to her, and that eventually she was going to crave the gift of life he needed to share with her. Her body was changing with each drop he took from her, though Josephine wasn't consciously aware of it.

No doubt the Snake Clan traitor had a mortal mother or grandmother who shared a bond with a Prime. A fully bonded pair were physically bound to each other, the shared blood providing nourishment for the Prime and extended life for the mortal. That it provided so much more was a private thing between the bonded.

And Gavin was even more ignorant of what it really meant to be a vampire than Brashear was. Granted, Gavin had a lot of self-confidence, a lot of cunning, and a lot of firepower he could call on.

But what was all that against the powers of a fully functioning Prime?

Marc was beginning to believe that he and Josephine had a chance. What they needed was a little more time—time for her mentally to accept what her body would soon want. He wasn't going to force his blood on her; she had to be ready for it.

"You're cautiously happy about something," his empathic lover said.

"Just high on life," he told her.

She grunted and sat up. He let her get out of bed and sat up himself to watch her walk across the room. "Nice butt," he called after her.

She paused and looked over her shoulder, her hands on her hips. She looked for all the world like an R-rated version of the famous Betty Grable pinup photo from World War II.

He responded with a wolf whistle.

She smiled at his response, and continued to sashay, her hips swinging, over to the refrigerator. She found some packaged meals in the freezer and popped two of them in the microwave.

"Those might be drugged," he warned, as the aroma of cooking meat wafted toward him. His stomach rumbled in response.

"Can you recall the last time you had solid food?" She reached into the refrigerator again and brought out pint cartons of milk.

She had a good point. He got up and came to sit at the table.

"You expect to be served, I see," she commented when she noticed where he was.

He shrugged.

"How a naked man can look so nonchalant, I do not know."

"I've spent a lot of time naked. What's for dinner?"

"Drugged meat loaf." She put a loaf of dull white sandwich bread on the table, along with a scattering of ketchup packets. Then she tossed him one of the milk cartons. The microwave timer sounded, and she turned to fetch the trays.

As she reached for the meals, he said, "Maybe the food isn't drugged. They won't want to contaminate your blood."

She turned back to him with an appalled look.

"After you drink mine," he added, bringing the subject out in the open.

Her spine stiffened, and every move she made showed her furious annoyance, from the way she took the meals out of the microwave to the way she slammed them onto the table and slapped her bare bottom down on the chair.

He peeled the covering back from his entree. As steam rose, he looked through it, and asked, "Did I say something wrong?"

She glared at him. "It's not a joke."

"It's my blood," he answered. "I certainly don't think it's a joke."

She made a face. "But—I can't do that!"

"Why not?" he asked with genuine concern.

"It's all right for you," she said. "You're used to it."

"Drinking blood?"

"Yes. Besides, I don't want to be a vampire."

"You won't be a vampire." He was pretty sure he'd mentioned this before, but maybe he hadn't explained it very well—or at all. Or maybe she hadn't been able to comprehend. Maybe she just hadn't been listening.

Whatever it was that blocked her acceptance, he tried again. "Drinking my blood won't make you a vampire. But the Patron wants—"

"To live forever," she interrupted. "I know that. What I don't understand is why they didn't just grab a female vampire and make her bite him. Wouldn't that solve his immortality fixation?"

Marc really wished she hadn't said that. He did his best to repair the damage, in case anyone was listening. "I'm sure Brashear's thought of that, and knows that it wouldn't work. Vampire females can only bond with vampire males."

That wasn't *exactly* true. Though it had once been forbidden, vampire women now sometimes took mortal lovers. It was true that they didn't bond with them in the same way Primes did with mortal females—the species might have died out long ago if they could—but the sharing of blood did halt the mortal male's aging process for as long as the relationship lasted.

Marc ate a few bites before he went back to the original subject. "We aren't going to get out of here until you do."

Josephine glared at him. "We get out of here in specimen jars if I do. No way am I doing anything to help that old creep."

He shrugged. "They're only going to give us so much time to do the deed on our own." He smiled, with a hint of fang in it. "You know you want to."

"I want more food," she said, and went back to the refrigerator.

Of course she did, and she wasn't hungry because of the blood he'd taken from her. That had been no more than a few drops during many hours of lovemaking. He was back in control of his intake, no longer needing her blood to heal.

"What you're hungry for is me," he told her.

She ignored this. "And I can't believe I just ate meat again without even thinking about it. You've corrupted me, Cage. There's some chocolate pudding. You want some?"

She turned around, holding a pair of sealed plastic cups. "That's not food," he said disdainfully. While he'd eaten greasy-spoon hamburgers and chicken out of necessity, and even enjoyed them, he was not about to eat prepackaged, chemical-laden junk food. "This body is a temple."

"More for me, then," she announced, and brought the pudding back to the table.

"I like what the cold air from the fridge does to your nipples," he informed her.

She ignored him, and they sat in silence while she polished off both containers. Someday he wanted to see that look of intense pleasure on her face when he served her *pot au chocolat*.

"Still hungry?" he asked, when she was done.

She sighed. "Yes."

He held out his arm, the wrist turned toward her.

She made a face. "Euwww." But she didn't look away. She stared avidly at his wrist, the color in her cheeks rising. He didn't think she was aware of licking her lips.

"The lady protests too much."

She bit her lower lip, then finally made herself look him in the eye. "What if I like it? What if I discovered I wanted to drink other people's blood?"

"Then you would be a slut," he answered gravely, "but you're not that kind of girl."

"I'm not going to become a bloodsucking creature of the night?"

Marc couldn't help but laugh. "No. That's my job."

"You're making fun of me."

He nodded. "A little. What we have is nothing to be afraid of, or ashamed of. Just the opposite."

"Gavin is playing you, messing with your head. He knew that if we were put in something like a normal setting, you'd—get all romantic and gentlemanly and want to get married, vampire style."

"Gavin knows me very well." *But not everything about me. Or you. Or what we will be together.*

She waved her arm at their prison. "It'll serve their purpose!"

"No," he said, standing. "It serves ours." He came around the table and took her by the hand. "Come on."

She held back when he urged her forward. "Where? What?"

"You said you wanted a shower," he reminded her, and tilted his head toward the bathroom.

Jo was totally confused by how calm he was,

how certain of the rightness of what he wanted of her. She had to admit that she did have a *craving* to share more with him. Logically, she knew it was a dangerous step into the dark. Emotionally, it was a passionate need to move away from being alone, move into a place of light and completion. It was a place where Marcus Cage waited for her, arms open, a place of acceptance, support, protection—for her, for him. Them.

"I really do love you, Cage." She sighed as they entered the bathroom. "I must be out of my mind."

He hauled her close, something that wasn't hard to do in the small space. "Do you love me despite a barbaric courtship? Or because of it?"

Jo rested her hands flat on his chest and looked up into his dark brown eyes. She didn't have to be an empath to sense how vulnerable he was at that moment, how hopeful and afraid.

"I don't know," she answered honestly. "You're you. You were desperate, and scary, but you were—nice. Kind. I understand now that you did what you had to do, trying to protect your people even more than you tried to protect yourself. You did the best you could."

He gave a mental sigh of relief as he drew her into a kiss. A gentle kiss at first, which quickly turned passionate and possessive. And not only on his part. After a few fiery moments Jo realized that she was digging her nails into his shoulders.

Was she trying to draw blood?

The fierceness rising in her frightened her, and she pulled away.

He accepted her reaction, but said, "You can't hurt me, Josephine. Not unless you don't love me."

He turned on the water and drew her into the shower stall. It was a very tight fit. The spray was hard and hot, and steam soon started to rise.

"Nice," she said. She picked up a tube of shower gel from the soap dish and squeezed it all over them. The scent of melon mingled with the steam. "What luxury," she murmured. She leaned back against his chest and closed her eyes as he washed her hair. She'd come to appreciate even the tiniest of luxuries, as well as the way this man mixed gentleness with strength. She knew so much about him, and yet there was so much more to learn. She longed to share all he was. And to share what she was with him. There were so many levels that beckoned, tantalizing, just out of reach . . .

"That feels so good," she said, as he began to massage her shoulders.

"You feel good." *In every way,* he whispered in her head.

She tried to relax, to live in the precious, peaceful moment. With the peace came clarity. The way he was touching her didn't distract her, but it did heighten her awareness of the—possibilities.

I feel—thirsty for you.

That was the only way to describe the ache inside her. Thirst for a sustenance that would feed her soul.

Then you're ready.

He turned off the shower and, with his arm around her waist, led her back into the other room. Their captors hadn't provided them with towels, so they ended up standing in the middle of the room, dripping water onto the painted cement floor. Jo barely noticed her wet skin growing cold in the air-conditioned room.

He held her out at arm's length. "You won't hurt me." He smiled, and anticipation glowed in his dark eyes. "You can count on that." *And don't be frightened when the guards come in. I'll take care of them.*

Jo blinked in sudden confusion and instant suspicion. She snatched her hands out of his. "What are you talking about? What gu—?"

He snatched her into a kiss before she could finish.

The Patron's mercenaries, he spoke into her mind. *The people holding us prisoner. They'll come for you as soon as you have my blood in you. To keep your blood uncontaminated, they won't use the gas. So they'll come in force when you've finished feeding.*

But—how would they know? Shit, Cage, have they been watching us?

Of course.

I checked for cameras; I'm not completely naïve. I didn't see any.

I haven't found them, either, but they must be there.

He was still kissing her, his tongue working wonders in her mouth. She was furious, and that fury was morphing into physical passion. If there was anybody watching, they were getting quite a show.

If? Why had she let herself pretend otherwise? That Cage had let her pretend was infuriating. When she thought about what they'd done—

It must have made watching X-rated porn seem tame.

And her actions weren't exactly prim and proper either. She was all over Cage with her mouth and her hands, and straining sinuous muscles, even while she mentally shouted, *You* knew *we were being watched—while we were screwing our brains out! How could you?*

For a hundred reasons. Because I love you. Because you love me. Because I need to make love to you and you alone. Because I needed sex and blood from a bondmate to regain my strength. With my full abilities back, we can escape.

You had sex with me as part of an escape plan?

You have something against escaping?

This last question knocked all the outrage right out of her. Of course she wanted to escape.

When we get out of here, I'm going to kill you.

His laughter filled her mind, and somehow his amusement soothed her ruffled feelings. *One thing at a time,* he thought. *First you have to drink my blood.*

"Fine." She realized that they were tangled up together on the floor like a pair of horny wet pretzels. She found the nearest patch of skin she was certain was his, and bit down.

"Ouch!" He bucked and pushed her off. He knelt beside her. "Not like that," he said, rubbing the tender spot above his navel.

Jo scrambled to her knees to face him. "How, then?" she demanded.

"I do the work."

She watched as razor-sharp fangs slid out over his lips. He lifted his left wrist to his mouth and sank his teeth into his own flesh. Blood welled from two punctures as he held his arm out toward her.

"Like this." He moved closer, and put his other hand around the back of her neck. "Lean forward," he urged. His deep voice was a rumbling, needy whisper. "Drink."

She couldn't take her eyes off the drops of hot, scarlet blood. The sweet scent of it called to her. She was past the point where she could stop herself from wanting it. Needing him.

Heart racing, she bent forward and touched her lips to his wrist. Lightning struck her then, fire from heaven. She was aflame, and so was he. She loved that he was there in the fire with her. They were two souls burning, two bright flames growing together, fusing into one raging inferno.

How long they were together in this private bright place, she had no idea. But nothing so intense could go on forever. Instinct told her that the completion was something to be returned to again and again, but that the world beyond was waiting. They would face the world side by side, stronger for what they experienced within this joining fire.

Though she didn't want it to end, when the fire died down to darkness, she accepted it with an utterly contented sigh.

"Welcome to my world, Mrs. Cage," was the last thing Jo heard before darkness completely took her.

Chapter Twenty-six

Mrs. Cage? Whoa.

It was her first thought upon waking from a brief nap. When Jo opened her eyes, she saw that she was lying on the floor between the bed and the wall. Then she heard the door crash open and people entering, and realized what was happening.

They'd come for her.

Cage had moved her to the one spot that afforded a small amount of shelter. It wasn't much, but it might delay them for a few seconds.

As she sat up, someone fired a shot. Instead of ducking back to the floor, Jo came to her feet, frantically looking around for Cage. All she saw was a blur of motion, and bodies flying as the blur passed by like the angel of death. She had to concentrate to make out the naked human shape of hard muscle and sinew and unnatural power that was the whirlwind.

Cage. She grinned.

A body flew toward her, and she jumped across the bed to avoid the man. He hit the wall with a thud and slid limply down it. Jo landed on the floor and stayed on her hands and knees as she watched Cage go through the guards like a warm knife through butter. Weapons were grabbed and tossed, bouncing with a hard metallic clatter off the walls. There were a few cries of pain.

"Amazing," she said, when he came to a standstill and was the only one standing. She got to her feet and did a quick body count. "There are seven of them. Are they dead?"

Cage turned to look at her, eyes glowing. "Does it matter?"

"Only if they're going to come after us."

"Come on," he said, heading for the door. "We haven't got much time."

Jo ignored him and knelt by one of the men, then quickly unbuttoned his shirt. "Help me," she said, when she had trouble lifting him to get the shirt off.

"What are you doing?"

"I'm not leaving here naked." She glanced at him. "I love your butt, City Mouse, but do you want it hanging out while we run for our lives?"

"Good point." Moving at high speed once more, he found the two downed guards who best approximated their sizes and stripped them.

Jo felt much better once she was dressed in baggy desert camo. One of the guards had been wearing sandals with Velcro closures, and she was able to adjust them to fit her feet. Cage loaded up on weapons and ammo, as well as getting dressed.

"Ready?" he asked, when she fastened the last sandal strap.

She picked up a pistol and stuffed bullet clips in her pockets. "Ready."

"Can you use that thing?"

"Yes."

"Will you?"

She crossed to the open door, paused, and looked cautiously up and down the white corridor. "Let's find out." And stepped out of their cell.

Marc admired Josephine's bravado, but he hurried to take the lead as they moved down the hallway.

"Hold up," he said, before they'd gone very far. "What do you sense?" he asked, when she stopped and gave him a worried look.

She closed her eyes, and he felt her shielding

open. She had more control than ever before. While they'd made love and he grew stronger, he had also taught her subconscious how to manage her strong empathic senses. As she sensed the outside world in her own way, he sensed it in his, tasting and scenting the air, and listening with hearing far more sensitive than mortal ears.

"Something's going on," they said together after a few moments.

"There's confusion," she said. "Worry. There's pain." She glanced back toward the cell. "Not just in here."

"Noise at the other end of the compound," he said. "A training exercise that's gone wrong, maybe. Whatever it is, we've got a diversion. Let's take advantage of it."

She nodded, and they hurried down the gleaming white corridor.

"This is too much like the dreams," she said, as they passed several doors.

He squeezed her shoulder. "I know. Only this time we get away." He willed her to believe it. They were armed, their captors were distracted. He was feeling fine.

"No dream," she said. "Not a drill."

They came to an intersection and automatically turned right. Then they paused and looked at each other. The exit they'd raced toward in the dream had been this way.

"It was only a dream." Josephine looked around worriedly.

This was no time to hesitate. "I trust my dreams," Marc answered. He took her hand. "Run," he ordered, the word spoken in a deep, commanding growl.

He ran, and she had no choice but to keep up with him. When a door opened as they approached it, Marc stopped long enough to break the neck of the freckle-faced man who appeared in the doorway.

"I know him," Jo said, staring at the crumpled body. He'd spoken to her at the meeting.

"Did he hurt you?" Cage asked.

She thought back to the medical tests they'd run on her. "Yes."

Marc nudged the body with his foot. "He won't anymore."

They hurried down the hallway again, reached a staircase, and raced down it.

At the bottom, Jo asked, "Was that gunfire?"

"Yes." It had been faint even to Marc's hearing. "Out near the west perimeter."

They went down another white corridor, this one shorter than the last, and at the end was a large, shining metal door.

"What is that stuff?" Jo asked. "Does the guy own a mithril mine?"

"It's pure silver," Marc answered. "I can't touch it." Not without third-degree burns. Even with his body chemistry returned to normal, it still wasn't possible for him to deal with so much of the deadly metal.

"It's not kryptonite," she complained.

He grinned. "Not to you." He stepped back and gestured her forward. "After you."

"Sure." She raised the pistol, shot the lock, and pushed at the door with the flat of her palms. "Heavy," she said as it slowly opened. "Must be worth a fortune. Wonder if it's solid silver or just a sheet of the stuff?"

"You planning on coming back and stealing the door?" he asked. "Wait." Before she could open the door farther, he jumped up and smashed all the lights near the door. When the area was dark he let her finish opening it. "Good. It's night."

"It's beautiful," she said.

Cool air flowed in from the outside, and distant noises came with it. Spotlights lit the compound and scattered buildings. Guards moved in the light, weapons at the ready. Marc and Josephine moved cautiously into the shadows by the wall of the building.

"What now?" she whispered.

Now—? "Steal a Hummer and smash through a fence, maybe? It doesn't have much of a chance, but—"

Josephine took in a sharp breath. "Wait a minute. How many people can fit in a Humvee?" she asked. "Will it take five?"

Marc looked at her in confusion. He didn't like the stubborn set of her jaw. "Five? Five what?"

"People. You, me, and the three women they brought in with us." She pointed to one of the buildings across the compound. "They're keeping them prisoner in there. We have to get them out."

"We? What? No."

"It's my fault they were captured. If I hadn't called my mom— Never mind how it happened, the point is, they're prisoners, too. If we escape, we have to take them with us. We have to help them."

"No, we don't."

Marc knew their chances were already small; if they tried to make this into a group outing, they were doomed.

"They'll kill them. They brought them here to feed you. If we're gone, they're excess baggage, liabilities. Do you really thing Gavin will keep them alive?" she demanded.

Marc very much wanted to tell her that the women were not his problem. She was the only one besides himself that he was obligated to take care of. Family took care of Family, and Josephine was now Cage of House Gianna of Family Caeg. The other women were mortals. He had no ties to them; they were—baggage, liabilities.

He looked across the compound, past the bright lights and patrolling guards. He shook his head. "I'd help them if it was feasible. It's not. Once we're free, we'll send back help."

She gave him a skeptical look. "If we get away, you know this base will be deserted before any help can get here."

Without further argument, she bent over and began to run a zigzag course across the compound. Marc had no choice but to follow.

The first bullet hit the ground at his heel, fired from one of the corner sentry towers. The splat it made as it impacted the hard surface told him it was soft metal. A silver bullet. Great.

He wouldn't have heard the second bullet if he hadn't been a vampire. It flew far over his head, fired at the sentry tower from a silenced gun. Marc heard the bullet impact in mortal flesh, the grunt of pain, and smelled the blood. He sensed the presence of another Prime, as well. He kept on running, fast enough to dodge any more bullets, flashed up to catch Josephine around the waist, and dragged her behind the shelter of a parked truck.

Within moments of his hauling his lady to the ground, the second vampire ran up to join them.

"Nice party," the new Prime said. He looked around with a wide grin, then back at Marc. "Are we having fun? Is that yours?" he added with a glance at Josephine.

The Prime had long dark red hair, dark eyes, a wiry build, a silenced rifle, and the overwhelming cheerful arrogance of a cocky young Prime. The cavalry had arrived, and Marc wondered if he was going to have to change its diapers.

"Who are you?" he asked.

The young Prime held up his left arm and showed the tattoo on the inside of his bared wrist. "Colin Foxe, Clan Reynard. When Terry and Annette got your message to us, I volunteered to come take a look."

"Terry and Annette?" Jo asked.

"The werefoxes," Marc guessed. One arm tightly around Josephine's waist, he told her, "I gave them a message to deliver to the Clan they're affiliated with. The message got through."

Colin Foxe smiled charmingly at Josephine. "I'm here to save you." He turned his attention back to Marc. "I actually just came in to scout around and report back to the Clan. But a sentry spotted me, so I figured I might as well do some damage while I'm here."

"Good thinking," Marc concurred. "That made a diversion for us."

"And I saved your life."

No young Prime was going to let that little favor pass. Marc nodded his gracious appreciation while Colin smiled past him at Josephine. Marc showed a bit of fang, just enough warning that he wasn't about to share his mate to show his gratitude for the Clan boy's assistance.

Colin gave a nonchalant shrug. They both knew he wouldn't be Prime if he didn't make at least a token effort to seduce, or in any other way acquire, a pretty sex partner.

"How's the baby?" Josephine asked.

"What baby?" Marc and Colin asked together, drawn out of their silent posturing.

"Terry and Annette's baby."

"I don't know," Colin answered.

"We don't have time for this," Marc said.

"Men," she complained.

"We have to get out of here," Marc said.

So far, none of the other guards in the compound had noticed them. The shooter had fallen from the tower when Colin shot him. Some had been drawn away toward where his body fell.

"We have to get to the women."

"Women?" Colin asked with great interest.

"The other prisoners," Josephine answered him. "Three women."

Oh, no. Marc closed his eyes for a moment. The last thing a chivalrous Clan boy needed to know was that there were other people who needed rescuing, and helpless women at that. Clan Primes lived for that kind of thing.

Colin rubbed a thumb along his jaw. "Going to be tricky getting three other mortals out."

"That's what I've been telling her," Marc said.

"Place is crawling with troops. I hiked in, but we'll need a vehicle to carry that many people. Access in and out is hard, even for SUVs. They can mount up a heavy-duty search operation."

"We know about that," Marc said.

"And they've got a couple of airplanes. So they can do aerial recon and—Planes!" he said, his face lighting up. He looked at Marc. "Can you fly one?"

Joy sparked through Marc like fireworks.

He should have remembered about the planes! He jerked a thumb at Josephine. "She's the pilot."

"I spotted a Gulfstream all fueled up and ready to go on the airfield," Colin said. "Can you fly it?"

"Yes," Josephine answered, followed immediately by a panicked, "No!"

"She can fly it," Marc assured the other Prime. He wanted to dance with joy. Instead, he rose to his feet and brought Josephine with him. "We're going home, Girl Scout."

"I—"

"I brought some explosives just in case I got the chance to blow up the lab you told the werefox about." Colin got up. "Where is it?"

Marc hated any delay in getting to the airfield, but he agreed that all the research data they'd amassed about vampires needed to be destroyed. And the scientists with it, with any luck. He pointed toward the lab building.

Colin gave a decisive nod. "You rescue the prisoners," he said. "I'll take out the lab and meet you at the plane." Then he sped off, his running figure a blur to any but vampire eyes.

Marc wanted to howl in frustration. He'd had enough of this prison. He wanted to go home.

He wanted his life back. Above all else, he wanted Josephine safe.

Then he looked at her, and she was looking at him with hope, admiration, and utter trust in her eyes.

He sighed. "All right. Fine. Let's go rescue the girls."

Chapter Twenty-seven

"I'm skinny," Jo said. "I think I can get through the window."

"Yeah," he said. "That'll work."

Staying in the dark as much as possible, they'd silently circled around to the back of the building where the women were being held. There were narrow windows high up in the wall. It had been decided that she should go in first and warn the women before Cage came barging in the door. After all, he'd already nearly frightened one of them to death. If the escape was going to go quickly and quietly, they didn't need screaming panic now.

Jo checked the safety on her gun, then stuck it in her waistband and looked around the ground near the wall. "Plenty of rocks. I need one big enough to smash the glass—here we are." She picked up a heavy rock and turned back to Cage.

"Give me a leg up," she requested.

The next thing she knew he grabbed her around the waist, and muttered, "Nobody tosses a dwarf." Then he tossed her.

She was able to grab on to the roof overhang, and plant a knee on the narrow window ledge. This gave her enough purchase to hang on with one hand while she hauled her other arm back and smashed the big rock into the window.

An alarm went off, of course, but Jo continued smashing broken glass until the hole was wide enough for her to slip safely through and ease herself down into the room.

When her feet touched the floor she quickly turned around and saw the three women huddled together by the table on the far side of the room. They stared at her in wide-eyed terror, but they didn't move or make a sound.

Then Jo looked over their heads and saw why. She shouted, "Marc, don't come—!"

But it was too late. The door smashed open, drowning out her warning.

Marc, duck! she thought belatedly.

Marc dropped to the floor in a shoulder roll

that took him to the center of the room. Though he dodged a bullet, the slug gouged a shard of concrete from the floor, which grazed Marc's cheek. *First blood to the enemy. How annoying.*

When he rose to his feet, he'd put his big body between Josephine and the man standing behind the trio of terrified hostages.

"Hello, Marcus," Jonas Gavin said from behind his human shields. "I knew this is where you'd come. You've always been soft-hearted."

Marc gestured toward Josephine. "Don't blame me. This is her idea." He glanced at the bullet that was lodged in the floor at his feet. "Silver."

"I thought it might get your attention."

"Must have terrible accuracy."

"It doesn't need much range close up. I could have shot you if I wanted to. Drop all your weapons."

He couldn't drop all of them—not the fangs, or claws, the speed or the strength, or the psychic talents—but he couldn't use them at the moment, either. One thing about humans, though, was their natural tendency to forget about supernatural abilities if you just behaved normally for a while. Marc did as he'd been told, slowly putting the weapons he'd taken from the guards on the floor, one by one.

Could he dodge a bullet, especially knowing what a fine marksman Gavin was? He put his hands up, showing that they were empty. Gavin kept the gun trained steadily on him.

"You don't want to shoot me, do you, Jonas?"

"I wouldn't mind, but that's not in the cards for right now."

"You're about to point out that I'm more valuable alive." Marc shook his head. "I'm through being a prisoner, Jonas."

Gavin smiled. It was an expression Marc was familiar with. When Gavin had that look, something appalling was about to happen. He grabbed one of the women lined up in front of him by the hair, and pulled her closer. He put the barrel of his gun to her forehead. "I definitely won't miss at this range."

"No!"

Marc put his arm out to catch Josephine when she shouted and rushed forward, and held her tightly around the waist. "No. You're the one he really wants. You're not getting close to him."

"Me? Oh, my blood."

"Come over here," Gavin called to Josephine.

"I'll let the women go. I'll even let Marcus go. We don't need him anymore."

Marc held on tight, so Josephine couldn't pull away and surrender herself for the sake of all of them.

She gave a short, cynical chuckle. "Like I'm going to believe anything you promise?"

Gavin looked surprised that his powers of persuasion weren't working. "Then I'll kill all of you."

"Better dead than a lab rat," Josephine answered.

"Good girl," Marc whispered to her. He let her go and put her behind him, retrieving the pistol tucked in her waistband.

Gavin shot at him even as Marc turned and lifted the gun.

If the explosion hadn't rocked the building at the same instant, Marc might not have been able to turn out of the bullet's path. As it was, it clipped his cheek and ear, splattering an arc of blood into his eyes. The lance of pain from the touch of silver drove him to his knees, and he dropped the pistol.

Outside the windows and broken door, the night lit with fire. The women screamed. Shattered glass fell like rain.

"Marc!" Josephine shouted above the din.

"Damn!" Gavin shouted.

Marc couldn't see for the blood, but his other senses told him where Gavin was. He followed body heat, scent, the vicious, angry emotions. He knew when the gun was turned on him again. And he moved with the speed of a vampire to reach his enemy before the weapon could harm him again.

There was a satisfying snap of broken bones when he grabbed Gavin's wrist and twisted it. Gavin's scream was the most gratifying sound he'd heard in a long time. Marc held on tight to Gavin with one hand, and wiped the blood from his eyes with the other. Then he held Gavin's head up and made the mortal look him in the eye.

Some vampires enjoy prolonging their enemy's death, he sent the thought into Gavin's mind. For a moment he let himself savor the wild burst of fear that erupted from deep in Gavin's twisted soul. *But you're not worth it.*

With that he broke Gavin's neck and turned back to the business of escaping as Gavin's lifeless body thumped to the concrete floor. For a long moment his gaze met Josephine's across the width of the room. He held his breath, not sure what to expect after she witnessed him killing someone. He knew his empathic mate had felt the death, and he didn't dare try to look into her mind.

She didn't look away from him, or flinch in horror. She was made of sterner stuff than that. She recognized the necessity of what he'd done and acknowledged it with a nod. She didn't even bother glancing at Gavin's body.

"Let's get this show on the road," she said, and paused only long enough to pick up her gun before crossing the room to the other women. "We're here to help," she told them.

One of the women was still screaming. The one Gavin had held the gun on was dazed and glassy-eyed. One of the women pointed at Marc. "He's the vampire!"

"Yeah," Josephine answered. "He's my vampire, and he's here to help you."

"But!" the woman shouted. "But, he's—!"

"A vampire. We all know that. And I," she added, "am the person now holding a gun on you. We don't have time for hysterics or arguments. Just get your asses out that door."

Marc crossed his arms and watched his woman in action, trying not to smile, which might ruin the effect of her performance if anyone looked his way. Not that any of these poor, scared women wanted to deal with a creature of the night. They probably preferred an angry woman with a gun in her hand giving the orders.

"Move!" the angry woman demanded, in a tone that would make a Marine sergeant proud.

The women moved, with Josephine bringing up the rear.

Marc beat them to the doorway and looked around. Across the compound, the lab was burning. The electrical generator must have been taken out, because the only light on the base now came from the conflagration. Just how much explosives had the Clan boy been carrying?

"Looks clear," he said, when the only troops he saw were those trying to fight the fire.

"Which way?" Josephine asked.

"Airstrip. We told Foxe we'd meet him at the plane."

Jo stopped in midstep, frozen with utter terror. "No."

"Yeah. That's what we told him."

She shook her head. "We'll take a Hummer."

Marc's hands landed on her shoulder. "We've been through this, my love. You are our best chance of getting all of us out of here."

The night swirled around her. "No," she whispered. She couldn't. "I can't fly."

"You want to fly," he told her. "You need to

fly." His deep voice was dark and honey sweet, seducing her to disaster. It took some doing, but Jo managed to focus her eyes on his face. His earnest expression hurt her, the hope and confidence that filled his emotions burned her. She had to swallow hard before she could get any words out of her fear-constricted throat. "You can't make me do this. Don't make me do this. I can't do this."

He pulled her close. She should have felt safe in the shelter of his arms, but she couldn't.

I can't make you, he thought. *I won't try to make you. But I know you can do it. You were born to fly.*

I'll get you all killed!

No, you won't.

He was so certain. So calm, and patient, and confident in her. It devastated her to know that she'd fail him.

You'll never fail me. And you won't fail yourself.

Marc dropped his arms and stepped away. He stood before her, a burning building at his back, and reminded her, "We haven't escaped yet. The Patron's mercenaries are going to remember about us at any moment. Foxe is risking his life to clear a path to the airstrip for us. Then it's up to you." He gestured toward the three women huddled together, then he held a hand out to Jo. "Time to go."

Up to me. Jo ran a hand through her short hair. *Up to me.* Her heart was trying to pound out of her chest, and she was covered in cold sweat. She hadn't been this frightened when Marc came rushing out of the darkness on that first night.

"Please!" one of the women cried. "You have to help us."

Damn!

Jo swallowed again. "Let's get to the airstrip," she told Marc.

Though she didn't know what was going to happen once they got there.

They found the young Prime standing in the shadow of the hangar entrance. "We have a bit of a crisis," was his greeting.

"You think?" Marc asked.

"It's not just the escape," Foxe answered. "Did you hear the other plane take off?"

"There were explosions, gunfire. I was in a fight. No, I didn't hear a plane."

"The twin engine," Josephine said, coming up beside him. "I thought I heard it."

"Yeah," Foxe agreed. "I managed to keep them away from the jet, but some of the guards managed to hustle an old man onto the other plane and get away."

"Old man?" Marc said. "Goddess—you let the Patron get away!"

"This is worse than I thought?" Foxe asked. "I destroyed the research, and as many of the researchers as I could find. The Snake breed is dead."

Marc frowned at the rude term, but let it go. It was up to the Matri and elders of their own clans to teach children manners. "But the boss got away," he explained to Foxe. "He's the one with the will and the financing."

"Who is he?"

"I have no idea. But we need to find out; he must be stopped."

Foxe put a hand on Marc's shoulder and looked at Marc with burning intensity. "Not we, Prime. Me. I let him get away. Besides, this is more Clan business than it is Family. It's the Clans that are supposed to safeguard the research."

"It is," Marc agreed. "But the Patron threatens all of our kind. Besides, shouldn't it be the Snakes that take the responsibility?"

"I know my Matri. She'd insist I finish what I started tonight, even if I weren't already decided on it. And she'll make sure the Snakes are involved in tracking down this Patron. You don't have to be in it if you don't want. You've been through enough. Besides . . ." He glanced toward Josephine. "I think you have other concerns in the next few months."

Foxe was right. He and Josephine were only at the beginning of their bonding processes. They needed a long, peaceful, intense time together.

Marcus gave the Clan Prime a nod. "Your hunt," he agreed. "But call me in at the kill if that's possible. I want to see this Patron taken down."

"Agreed."

Jo stood apart from the men, not really paying attention to their conversation. There was shouting in the distance and occasional gunfire, though she had no idea what the mercenaries were shooting at. Seeing phantom vampires everywhere, she supposed. And the noise, and the danger that came with it, was growing closer.

She jumped when Marc came up and touched her on the shoulder. "Time to go," he whispered, leaning close to her ear.

"I'm cold," she said, staring at the sleek, small jet sitting nearby on the end of the dark runway.

Dark wouldn't be a problem; it was the kind of airplane that came fully loaded with every kind of instrument money could buy. And it was prepped for takeoff, or the Patron's staff wouldn't have tried to board it. All she had to do was walk into the cockpit, sit down in the pilot's seat, and let her hands and eyes do what they'd been trained so well to do. It meant freedom and safety for them all. Above all else, Marcus Cage deserved freedom and safety. If only she could give it to him.

"I'm cold," she said again.

"I'm here," he said. But he didn't touch her. He didn't make promises, or give reassurances, didn't tell her she was brave and he knew she could do it. He stood at her side, and waited.

"Dammit," she said at last, giving him a hard, angry glare. Then she took a step, then another, approaching the jet with the same trepidation she would a fire-breathing dragon.

The women followed, with the other vampire running ahead to enter the plane first. "Clear," he called from the doorway.

Jo watched Marc shepherd the other women forward. She was tempted to turn and run, but they needed her. Marc needed her.

What if she got them killed?

Gunfire sounded close behind her, and concrete and sparks flew as bullets hit the ground nearby.

That was her answer.

She ran the last few steps onto the jet. Once on board she sprinted through the luxurious cabin, barely aware of the people already strapped into seats, and heard Foxe securing the bulkhead door.

Marc stood by the cockpit entrance. "Anything I can do?"

"Stand by this door and don't let me come out."

"Deal."

She couldn't help but smile at the sound of his deep voice, and she turned that smile on him. "Thanks."

He pointed. "Go."

Shaking like a leaf, she faced the open door, saw the arc of instruments and the runway stretching off into the night beyond the cockpit window. She was about to enter the dragon's mouth, indeed.

"Wait a minute," she said, turning abruptly around.

"Where are we? Where are we going? I can get us in the air, but I need some reference points."

"This used to be Fort Copeland, if that's any help," Foxe called from the back of the plane. "My Clan has a private airport on the Salton Sea. I can get you there, but get us airborne now!"

Jo's roiling nerves settled a little. She knew

exactly where Fort Copeland was. This time she didn't hesitate in entering the cockpit. She walked into her world and settled firmly into the pilot's seat. She glanced back once, and Marc blew her a kiss and closed the cabin door.

She ran her gaze and her hands over the familiar controls. Now she was alone. No, she had Marcus Cage with her. Always. "Sort of like the Force," she muttered.

She brought the power up on the engines, loving the fine-tuned hum that turned into a full-throated dragon's roar. She could ride this dragon. Though she was still afraid, a thrill of anticipation sang through her, as well. She'd missed this!

She wanted this. She looked up at the stars overhead. Her heart reached for the sky, and her hands moved, knowing how to take her there.

Marc should have been strapped into a seat, but he waited on his side of the door. His hands were pressed to the cool metal surface, his eyes closed, his concentration completely on the woman he loved. She was in a place where he couldn't help her, but he was there with her. Her fear pulsed through him, then longing took her, and love. The plane began to roll down the runway. He became aware of speed. With the speed came a singing, yearning pleasure.

Then joy burst through her—them—and the plane leapt into the air.

"Yiihaaa! Yes!" Josephine's shout burst out of the cockpit, just as Marc was thrown backward by gravity onto the deck.

He put his head back and laughed with joy, loving her, feeling pretty triumphant himself.

"Yes!" He punched a fist in the air.

They were going to be all right.

Epilogue

Six Weeks Later

"There is nothing more comforting than a long, hot bath. And bubbles makes it even better."

A pair of full champagne flutes in her hands, Jo looked across the vast expanse of rosy marble, crystal, and gold that was their hotel suite's bathroom. Marc grinned at her from the depths of the huge sunken tub. Candles gleamed on the wide marble shelf behind him, lending gold accents to his curly black hair. He was covered up to his broad, bare chest in a rich foam of bubbles. Cinnamon-scented steam rose from the hot water.

"On you, that looks good," she told her husband.

She supposed that technically he was her bondmate. He wasn't going to be her husband until tomorrow afternoon.

"You look like Venus being reluctant about coming out of the sea," she told him.

She crossed the room, loving the feel of the cool tiles on her bare feet and the silky touch of her peacock blue robe against her skin. When she handed him his glass of champagne their fingers touched, and hot pleasure shot through her. Their gazes met.

He said, "You could climb in here with me, and we could *try* to make it a quick one."

It was very tempting, but she took a step back and took a sip from the flute. Marc, who knew a lot about such things, had assured her it was excellent champagne. She liked the taste, but being with him like this made her giddy without any help from the wine.

"You have to come out sometime," she told him. "Come on," she coaxed, letting the silk slide seductively off one shoulder. "My mom's not that scary."

He arched an eyebrow at her, though his gaze was riveted on what she'd revealed of one breast. "Your mother ran a make on me for priors."

Jo shrugged, revealing a bit more skin. "She does that on all my boyfriends."

"I'm not a boyfriend."

"She was a little leery of you at first. You can't blame her, when we showed up with a wild story about thwarting a forced prostitution ring led by that corrupt sheriff in Kennedyville."

"She believed us. And the ladies we rescued corroborated the story."

"After you hypnotized everyone. Which *was* safer for everyone involved and makes a lot more sense than the truth," she admitted.

"The investigation found plenty of evidence about the sheriff's bad deeds."

Apparently there were experts among vampire kind that specialized in operations that kept the vampire world invisible from mortal kind. She didn't blame them for their secrecy, not after what happened with the Patron. She still had nightmares.

And Marcus was there to comfort her every time she woke up with one. And she was there for him.

And now they were getting married tomorrow. And he'd taken her to Venice—sort of. They were staying at the Venetian hotel in Las Vegas, and getting married in the wedding chapel at the hotel. She'd spent a busy few days crisscrossing the country, flying in relatives and friends from both sides. She'd relished every minute spent in the air, even as she'd missed Marc dreadfully when away from him. He'd been putting the finishing touches on the restaurant he was opening in Vegas, getting it ready in time for the wedding reception to be held there tomorrow night.

They had their lives back, they had their careers, they had the magic of the bond, and they had each other. When he'd captured her that night in the desert, she couldn't have imagined it would lead to this.

"Perfection," she said.

"You are," he agreed.

She turned toward the nearest mirror and marveled at the scars that were fading. She also marveled at the lack of pain. She hadn't realized how much physical and emotional pain had become a part of her life, until he began to heal her. Tomorrow she'd be wearing a strapless wedding gown covered in lace and crystal beads. And to think that a few weeks ago, she'd been reduced to wearing stolen combat fatigues.

"We've had quite a ride, Mr. Cage."

"Indeed we have, Mrs. Cage." As she turned back to him, he added, "Let's not do it again. Now, about my mother-in-law's distrustful attitude—"

"Hey, you didn't have a record—she likes you now."

He sipped champagne and put the glass down on the wide rim of the tub. "You have a strange family."

"In comparison to what? Yours? I like your family," she added. "Even if your great-grandmother's a little scary."

"She has to be. She's the Matri. She needs to be tough to keep the Family in line."

"And I understand why. Your young male relatives are—a lively bunch. If they keep hitting on my sister, somebody's going to get hurt. And it won't be Officer Friendly Phillipa Elliot."

"Josephine *and* Phillipa—your father wanted all boys, didn't he?"

"They're family names. From a grandmother on each side, and my brother is Matthew Elliot III, after Dad and Grandpa. My family has as many traditions as yours."

"Yeah." He smiled fondly. "I like that about them. I like the way your nipple's puckering, too. You want to come here and let me play with it?"

She took a teasing step backward and shook her head. "I told you you had to come to me. And we don't have time to fool around." She pulled the robe back up and tightened the belt. "I'm not going to be late for the rehearsal dinner."

"My family will understand."

"They're all sex fiends."

He stood up in the bathtub, looking more like Mars rampant arising from the foam than Venus. She glanced at his erection. "Correction. You're all sex fiends."

"Famous for it," he answered, and came to her. It wasn't long before they were making love on the bathroom floor. A quick, happy, wet bout of sex that left them breathless, laughing, and utterly satisfied.

"We better get dressed," he said, after they finished up with a shower that was only slightly quicker than their lovemaking. He took her hand and led her out of the bathroom.

Marc continued on through the living room into the suite's bedroom. Jo came to a halt in front of a low table, staring at the beautifully wrapped box resting next to a huge vase that contained many white roses and one red one.

"What's this?" she called after Marc.

"For you," he called back. "Open it."

Jo touched the roses first and buried her face in the soft blossoms. She nearly became drunk on the sweet scent, and smiled at knowing that roses had thorns. It was all very symbolic, and sweet as well.

Marc came back into the living room, dressed all in black. His powerfully built body was shown off to perfection by the beautifully tailored suit and black silk shirt. She loved the way his curly black hair framed his face.

"Don't stare at me, woman," he said. "Open your present."

She held up the box, wrapped in silver paper and tied with gold ribbon. The bow was as big as a plate. She shook it. "It's so pretty, I hate to."

He folded his arms, and used his Sergeant Cage voice. "Open it."

She grinned and tore into the wrapping. Within moments she put the box on the table, and lifted the white cardboard lid.

When she saw what was inside, she began to laugh. "Good God," she said, taking out one T-shirt after another. *"Adrenalize, Hysteria, X, On through the Night."* She looked at him. "They're all here, aren't they?" He nodded. "Even some I didn't have before."

She laid out the Def Leppard tour shirts in a fan pattern. Being named Jo Elliot, a name almost exactly the same as the British rock band's singer, Joe Elliot, had gotten her a lot of Def Leppard paraphernalia as gifts over the years. She really wasn't that much of a fan of the band, but she'd become sentimentally attached to her shirt collection.

"You found all of them?"

"eBay is my friend," he answered. "You lost your collection saving me. I wanted you to have them back."

"Jo Elliot thanks you." She grabbed him close and kissed him. *And Josephine Cage adores you.*

POCKET STAR BOOKS
PROUDLY PRESENTS

PRIMAL HEAT

Available in paperback
from Pocket Star Books

Turn the page for a preview of
Primal Heat. . . .

"*Y*our in-laws are scary," Phillipa Eliot told her sister, who was a lovely and not-in-the-least blushing bride.

Phillipa leaned against the terrace railing next to her sister, and took another sip of very good champagne. The hot wind that blew in off the desert didn't bother her. Heck, she was from Phoenix; there was no way Las Vegas could get hotter than home. The dry air did make her thirsty, though; she thought she was on her fifth glass of champagne.

Josephine's eyes went wide. "What do you mean by scary?"

Phillipa looked at the people dancing at the wedding reception in the hotel ballroom. "They make me feel like I've crashed the supermodels' annual ball."

Jo laughed. "Yeah, I know exactly what you mean." Her gaze didn't leave her new husband, who was currently dancing with their mother. "Isn't he—?"

"Large," Phillipa cut in.

"I was going to say cute."

Phillipa laughed. "Of course you were."

She thought that the hulking groom was probably the least handsome man there. Not that the muscular Marcus Cage didn't have enough charm and charisma for three normal males. It seemed to run in the Cage family, and among all their friends. The women were amazingly beautiful, mostly in a dark and mysterious way. And the men—good lord!

They'd been hitting on her since the rehearsal dinner the night before. It had been quite a stimulating experience.

Phillipa took a moment to fan her face. She wasn't sure if it was the champagne, or the mere thought of the men at the reception that was causing the warmth that stirred through her. There was something special about this bunch; after all, she was a cop and used to working around hunky, hard-bodied, macho men. Not only was she used to it, she liked it. But the Cages and their friends had so much going for them in the confident, sexy male department that they were downright daunting.

"It's not that I don't like the Cage clan," Phillipa explained.

"Family," Josephine said. "They're a family, not a clan."

"What difference does that make?"

Jo laughed. "Never mind, and I can't explain anyway. If I did, they'd probably have to kill you. It's a joke between Marc and me," she added quickly.

Phillipa let it go. Far be it from her to try to interpret the private language of newlywed lovebirds, especially after five glasses of champagne.

She looked at her empty glass, and said, "I'm switching to water." One of the groom's hunky relatives was heading their way, and his gaze was fixed on her. "Right now," she added, and left so he'd have to ask her sister to dance instead of her.

The band stopped playing as she skirted the dance floor and she noticed Marc heading for Jo, and Mom heading toward where Dad waited for her. Phillipa smiled, appreciating the devotion of the happy couples. At the same time, she had to fight off a twinge of sadness at being alone herself. She blamed the self-pity on the champagne, because she had no one to blame for breaking up with Patrick but Patrick. You'd think with all the gorgeous men in the place, she'd be more interested in hooking up with one of them.

Maybe I don't want another macho man. Maybe that was why all the groom's male relatives set off alarm bells she couldn't explain.

The band started playing again as she reached the bar.

"Not more Queen," a man said behind her.

The disgust in his voice amused her, and the deep British accent was intriguing. As the band continued with "Another One Bites the Dust," she took the water the bartender handed her, then turned around. She hadn't noticed the man standing behind her before, though she was somehow aware of his presence before he spoke. His hair was wavy and sandy brown, his eyes green and surrounded by laugh lines. He had a lived-in face; a dangerous face.

"I know what you mean," she told him. "If they play 'Fat-Bottomed Girls,' I'm out of here."

"I'll join you," he answered.

"And if they start playing a lot of Def Leppard, Jo will run away screaming."

Phillipa moved away from the crowd surrounding the bar. The newcomer followed after her as she edged around the dance floor on her way back to the terrace.

"Who's Jo, and what's wrong with Def Leppard? I'm a proud son of Sheffield myself," he added.

"Where's that?"

"Northern England. Same hometown as the Lep—?"

"And what do you mean, who's Jo?" Phillipa stopped and confronted him. "You *are* a guest at the Elliot-Cage wedding, aren't you?"

His smile was devastating, showing deep dimples and crinkling the lines around his eyes. "I'm the best man."

Irritation flared over the heat that had been

roused by his smile. "You're Matt Bridger!" she accused. "You very nearly ruined this wedding!"

"It's not my fault my plane was late."

"You were supposed to have arrived yesterday."

He gestured at the boisterous people filling the crowded room. "It doesn't look like I was missed."

"One of my brothers stepped in as best man."

"Then it all turned out all right." He crossed his arms over his wide chest, and moved close to her. "I don't know what you have to be angry about."

"I'm angry on my sister's behalf."

"Why's that?"

"She's Jo Elliot."

"The singer in Def Leppard?"

"The bride!"

Even as she indignantly declared this, Phillipa realized that Matt Bridger was perfectly aware of it, and that he was teasing her.

She stepped closer to him. Suddenly they were toe to toe and nose to nose. He put an arm around her waist, drawing her even closer. She was caught by the masculine heat and scent of him. "You're provoking me on purpose."

The back of his hand brushed across her cheek. "Yes."

Her knees went weak and she almost dropped her glass. She didn't notice where it went when he took it out of her hand.

"Dance with me."

"Yes."

And she never wanted to dance with anyone else.

He drew her onto the dance floor, and they started dancing slowly to the fast music. It was the most natural thing in the world to gaze into this stranger's eyes and press her body against his, soft and hard blending. They didn't share a word while the music played, yet the communication between them was deep and profound. She'd known him forever, been waiting for him forever. It was all too perfect to make any sense.

When the music stopped she would've kept right on dancing, but Matt turned them off the dance floor. Her arms stayed draped around his wide shoulders and her gaze stayed locked with his. His palms pressed against the small of her back, large and warm and possessive.

Despite this intimate closeness, Phillipa tried to regain her sanity.

"We've just met."

"And you're really not that kind of girl."

"What kind of girl?"

"The sort who snuggles up to a stranger the moment they meet. And I'm not that sort of man." He flashed that devastating smile at her again. "Mostly."

"Then why are we—"

"We have more than snuggling in mind."

"Yes, but—"

"I have a theory."

She didn't want to hear his theory. "Kiss me."

Fingers traced across her lips. "Soon."

His touch left her sizzling. This was crazy! She should be embarrassed. Phillipa took a deep breath and made an effort to step away. She managed to move maybe an inch, a small triumph for public decency.

"Like calls to like," he said, pulling her back to him.

She lost interest in decency. "I'm a cop."

"Fancy that." As the music started again, he took her by the hand. The connection was electric. "Come on."

She held back. This was her last chance to stay virtuous. "I don't—"

"Listen."

She did, and laughed. "Oh my God, 'Fat-Bottomed Girls.'"

"You said you'd leave if they played it."

"Left alone with big fat Fanny—she was such a naughty nanny . . ." sang the band.

"Matt Bridger, let's get out of here."

They headed toward the door, but he stopped after a few steps. "One thing, first."

"What?"

"Your name."

"Phillipa Elliot."

At least she wasn't about to fall into reckless abandon with a *total* stranger, now.

He tilted his head and gave her a quick, thorough once-over. What he saw was a tall blond woman in a strapless tea-length teal satin bridesmaid's dress.

"I know, I don't look like a Phillipa," she said. "But who does?"

"Pardon me for saying so, but that is an unfortunate name for a Yank, isn't it?"

"I'm used to it."

"Good. It suits you."

The band started in on the chorus again, and they ran for the door.

They didn't kiss until they were in the elevator, coming together in a rush of heat. His mouth was hard and demanding on hers, and she responded just as fiercely. The way he caressed her made her feel naked despite the satin dress and layers of undergarments. His fingers tracing along her bare shoulders and the back of her neck drove her wild. She knew this was crazy, but she didn't care.

Until she noticed that her skirt was hiked up around one hip and his hand was stroking the inside of her thigh. It felt wonderful.

"We're not exactly private here," she reminded him. "Hotel"—she gasped as his fingers moved higher—"security."

"Room key," was his answer.

He stopped long enough for her to fumble

open her tiny purse, and the doors slid open onto the fourteenth floor just as she pulled out the black plastic key card.

"This is it." She didn't remember pressing the button for her floor, but she hadn't told him where her room was. Odd. At least the room wasn't far from the elevators, and they were there within a few moments.

Inside, he whirled her around onto the bed.

"You make me dizzy," she said as he leaned over her and she looked into his green eyes.

"Only dizzy?"

There was a wicked glint in those eyes, and a world of sensual promise in his slight smile. There was also something dangerous about his deep, slightly rough voice. The sound of it sent a thrill through her.

"Say something else."

He chuckled. "What is it about Yank women and English accents?"

"Don't complain if it helps you get laid," she told him.

He laughed again. "Would this sound seductive in Sheffield?" he asked, doing a very good job of mimicking an American accent.

"Yes. But it's not just your accent that's sexy. You have gorgeous lips," she added. When she traced them with a finger, he nipped it. "And sharp teeth."

"Oh, yes." He kissed her throat.

Her blood raced as warm lips pressed against her tender skin. His hand brushed across the satin covering her breast, sparking the overwhelming desire to have his naked flesh against hers.

A moment later he tugged her to her feet and pulled on the dress's long zipper. As the dress pooled around her feet, his thumb slid slowly down the length of her bare spine. She arched against him.

"Skin on skin, just like you want," he murmured. His lips were close to her ear. Then they were on her throat.

There was a moment of sharp pain, followed by blinding ecstasy. When her mind cleared from the blissful overload, they were back on the bed once more, and he was as naked as she was. She ran her hands across his chest, and appreciating the sight and texture of hard muscles and hot flesh.

"You are so sweet," he told her.

"I'm more than sweet." She pulled his head down and kissed him hard.

"You're also hot," he agreed.

He kissed her gently, on the lips and on the cheek. But she was aware of the edge of ferocity he was holding back. Then his head moved down and his tongue swirled around one hard nipple, and then the other.

She moaned, and inside the needy sound she heard his voice. *I'm trying to stay civilized.*

Don't, she answered.

His touch grew rougher then, and her responses were just as frantic. He kissed and bit her all over. Each pinprick of pain that followed the soft brush of lips brought her a flash of mounting pleasure.

The contrast was maddening. Wonderful.

With each flash, the heat pooling in her belly grew and spread until the orgasms became one long, continuous wave of ecstasy. She didn't think it could get better—until he was inside her, filling her with hard, fast strokes that drowned her in fiery sensation. She clung to him, rose to meet him with the same frantic energy, wanted nothing but more.

More was what he gave her. She gave herself up to him, blended with him, blood, mind and soul, and he gave himself to her. She was complete with him, whole with him, until one last, shattering explosion sent her over the edge and into darkness.

"That was—" Phillipa sighed, unable to describe the experience. Now she understood why sex was called The Little Death. Maybe only good sex was called that. Great sex.

Little sparks of pleasure were still shooting through her. She was exhilarated and exhausted at the same time. She was completely content to come back to reality to find herself lying across

Matt, with her breasts pressed against the hard muscles of his bare chest. She rested her cheek against the warmth of his skin, and breathed in his male scent.

"It certainly was," Matt answered.

He was lying on a pile of pillows, his hands propped behind his head, a smug smile curving his beautiful mouth. She caught the sparkle of green in his half-closed eyes.

"You look like a well-fed cat," she told him.

"Very well-fed," he answered. "But still hungry."

He pulled her up the length of his body for a kiss. His mouth was as insistent and needy as if they hadn't just made love. As his hands began to roam, he made her hungry all over again.

This time she was able to keep her head long enough to say, "Maybe we shouldn't." His mouth circled a nipple. "Oh, God! I mean— there's supposed to be photos—and—wedding stuff." She was too deep into the pleasure to remember just what. "We'll be missed."

He nuzzled her, and his voice was muffled from between her breasts. "Do you really care?"

"Nooo—yes! We'll be missed. I should be there. She's my sis—" She suddenly became very aware of his erection, and her hand closed around it. She had to touch him, to stroke him. "I shouldn't be doing this."

"You better not stop."

His hungry growl sent a needy shiver through

her. His voice was enough to make her melt. "But—"

This sort of thing happens at family gatherings all the time.

"What happens?"

People disappear to make love. It's a way to celebrate the bonding.

"That's nice." It occurred to Phillipa that there was something odd about this conversation. "Did you just say something inside my head?"

Not that you'll recall. Relax, sweetness. Make love to me.

"All right." It was all she wanted to do anyway.

A carousel music version of "Ode to Joy" woke Phillipa up, but her first thought was, *I belong with this man.* When she came a little further awake she realized that the noise was a cell phone ringing, and that she was lying naked in a dark hotel room with Matt Bridger. She couldn't think of anywhere better to be, and snuggled closer to him while Beethoven kept playing.

Eventually Matt grunted and rolled over to pick the phone up from the nightstand. "Mike, if you're drunk, you're a dead lobo." Whatever the answer was, it made Matt sit up. His muscles bunched with tension. "Where and when? Right. I'm not alone."

Phillipa decided to let him ride out this emergency in privacy, and took the opportunity to slide out of bed for the bathroom. She took her time using the facilities and drinking a glass of water.

As she stepped back into the dark bedroom she was aware of its emptiness. The musky tang of sex was still in the air—but even before she turned on a light and saw the rumpled, empty bed, she knew he was gone.